"I know how passionate you are, remember."

Liam watched as a tide of hot color flowed up to Suzy's hairline. "Yes," he whispered, "I remember, too." He stared at her quivering mouth and to her shame she felt it part. Liam bent his head suddenly and his kiss softly ran along the curve of her mouth, his hands touching her intimately, caressingly.

In spite of her knowing the contempt he felt as he touched her, Suzy's whole body came alive under his fingers. She felt her lids come down, her spine arch. Liam's mouth closed over hers and they kissed.

Then he lifted his head and laughed. "As I suspected," he whispered. "I could still have you if I wanted you." He watched her face stiffen and burn, smiling at her, deliberately insulting her. "But you see, I don't."

CHARLOTTE LAMB began to write "because it was one job I could do without having to leave the children." Now writing is her profession. She has had more than forty Harlequin novels published since 1978. "I love to write," she explains, "and it comes very easily to me." She and her family live in a beautiful old home on the Isle of Man, between England and Ireland. Charlotte spends eight hours a day working at her typewriter—and enjoys every minute of it.

Books by Charlotte Lamb

A VIOLATION
SECRETS

HARLEQUIN PRESENTS

HARLEQUIN ROMANCE

Don't miss any of our special offers. Write to us at the following address for information on our newest releases.

Harlequin Reader Service
901 Fuhrmann Blvd., P.O. Box 1397, Buffalo, NY 14240
Canadian address: P.O. Box 603,
Fort Erie, Ont. L2A 5X3

CHARLOTTE LAMB

LAMB

kiss of fire

Harlequin Books

TORONTO • NEW YORK • LONDON
AMSTERDAM • PARIS • SYDNEY • HAMBURG
STOCKHOLM • ATHENS • TOKYO • MILAN

Harlequin Presents first edition January 1988
ISBN 0-373-11042-1

Original hardcover edition published in 1987
by Mills & Boon Limited

CHAPTER ONE

SUZY saw the pyramid of books across the aisle in the station bookshop and froze in her tracks. She had come in to hunt for a magazine to read in the train, going down to Romney Marsh for the weekend, an idea shared by a number of other passengers, obviously, because the shop was crowded, and as Suzy stopped dead someone ran into the back of her, giving a grunt of irritation.

'Sorry!' Suzy said automatically without looking at the middle-aged man pushing past her.

'Excuse me!' he snarled, glaring, but she didn't really notice because her eyes were riveted by the cover of the top book in the pyramid balanced on a low table. The artwork was that of a children's comic: vivid colours, simple lines, everything about it exaggerated and immediate. It was very effective; two racing cars seemed to be about to leap out at you, one of them just crashing, exploding into flame.

That, in itself, was enough to make the hair stand up on the back of her neck; but it was the author's name that really shook her. It ran across the top of the cover in bold, black lettering, a name which once dominated headlines but which she hadn't seen for a very long time. She had wondered from time to time what Liam Moor was doing; now she knew. He had been writing a book.

'The train now arriving at Platform Six is the eleven forty-seven for . . .' The muffled voice of the tannoy cut through her thoughts; she looked at her watch with a start—that was her train, she would have to hurry.

She picked up a magazine, then hesitated, looking back at the pyramid of books. Every instinct warned that she shouldn't buy a copy. It was stupid even to consider reading it, when simply to see his name conjured him up in front of her—hard grey eyes, sardonic smile, restless body; Liam's image was as destructive as guilt. If she was wise she wouldn't let him touch her life again. You couldn't rewrite the past—it had happened and couldn't be altered—but you could forget it if you avoided anything that might awaken memories, she reminded herself.

She turned towards the cash desk, then swung round again, almost knocking over someone starting to queue up behind her. It was the same man who had cannoned into her a few moments ago, but Suzy was unaware of that, throwing a polite smile to him with her murmured, 'Sorry.'

'Why don't you make up your mind whether you're coming or going or just standing in everyone else's way?' he burst out, red-faced and glowering. 'You women are all the same!'

Suzy looked at him, blue eyes wide and astonished, quite at a loss.

'Women!' he growled, leaning towards her.

Suzy fled and found herself beside the pyramid of books, as if her feet had taken her there without her mind having an idea where she was going.

She picked up a copy and hurried back to the cash desk before she could change her mind. The black girl behind the till gave her a conspiratorial grin.

'You're safe; he's gone. I thought he was going to burst a blood vessel, bad-tempered old man!'

Suzy smiled weakly, paying her. 'Maybe he quarrelled with his wife this morning.'

As the train left the station, she opened the book, intending to skim a few pages, but Liam's style was too easy to read; it dragged her onwards, the words crisp, rapid, almost journalistic. She was unaware of the endless grey ribbon of suburban streets stretching out from London into the sunlit Kent countryside, blind to the other people in the compartment, the brief stops at other stations on the line. Her hands clenched on the cover, trembling and icy.

It hadn't occurred to her that he might have written an autobiographical novel, even though the cover made it clear that he had used the racing background he knew so well. Liam had changed the facts, disguised them cleverly enough to fool most people, but Suzy knew that she was the girl in the book. Wincing, she read on, hating him.

She almost missed her station, so engrossed in what she was reading that she didn't look up as the train pulled to a halt. A man seated opposite got up and dropped a briefcase on her lap. Startled, Suzy raised wide blue eyes as he apologised, then she glanced at the station platform and saw the name with a shock. The other passenger opened the carriage door and climbed down, and Suzy grabbed her suitcase and almost fell out after him.

Sara Stevenson was waiting for her at the ticket barrier, her auburn hair glittering in the sunlight as she waved. Suzy waved back, banishing the bleakness of reading Liam's book. She would think about that later, when she was alone.

'How's the invalid?'

'Having a whale of a time,' Sara said, taking her suitcase. 'The car's just outside. Did you have a comfortable journey? That train seems to take forever, doesn't it?'

Sara's husband, Alex Stevenson, had picked up some unknown bug while he was filming in Hong Kong some weeks earlier. Suzy had been out there with the film crew; she had had to cable Sara with the news that Alex was very ill; she had met her at the airport and driven her straight to the hospital. Suzy knew how distraught Sara had been when she first saw Alex. He had been delirious and hadn't known his wife, and Sara had sat at his bedside crying while Suzy tried to comfort her. For days Alex had hovered between life and death and the two women at his side had grown closer every day. They hadn't known each other very well until then, but during the crisis of Alex's illness they had become friends.

'He sounded very restless on the phone,' Suzy said, climbing into the passenger seat of Sara's red Ford.

'That was yesterday. Some days he can't wait to get back to work and fidgets around like a two-year-old, but the doctor's adamant about keeping him in bed for at least another week, most of the time anyway. He's allowed to get up for an hour today. If that does no harm, it can be two hours tomorrow, and so on.'

'I bet Alex loves that!'

'He's been driving me crazy,' Sara agreed, mouth wry as she moved off. They took a narrow, winding road between hedges .just breaking into new leaf; catkins swung in a spring breeze, shedding a drifting dust. The countryside was flat and secretive, occasionally pierced by a church steeple or a fleeting glimpse of the blue-grey sea. Suzy considered it all without real enthusiasm; she was a city girl to her fingertips, having been born in London and lived there all her life. She loved the smell of petrol fumes and Indian take-aways, the snarl of taxis and the hooting of cars, the rumble of lorries, the permanently lit shop windows, day and night, the feel and sound of a great city all around you. She knew that she would find life in this remote landscape more claustrophobic than peaceful, but Sara seemed to spend all her time there, and almost never came up to London.

'Mr Jonas thought Alex might be keen to get back to work . . .' she began, and Sara exploded.

'Oh, did he? Well, of course he's right, but Alex isn't nearly fit enough, and I wish L.J. would mind his own business. I want to talk Alex into having a couple of weeks in the sun somewhere, but if L.J. gets at him I won't have a chance.'

'I'm sure Mr Jonas wouldn't do anything to delay Alex's recovery,' Suzy said quickly and soothingly. 'He just thought Alex might like to read a few scripts while he's resting.'

'The thin end of the wedge,' muttered Sara, scowling. She was a volatile, emotional redhead with

slanting green eyes and a figure that made men stare.
Suzy often envied her those dramatic looks; they
were very different types and Suzy didn't have that
sort of impact on the opposite sex.

'Well, I've brought a pile of letters with me, and a
telex from Mr Jonas, from Los Angeles; he says he'll
be home on Thursday and will be down to see Alex
that weekend.'

'I wish I could get Alex away by then,' Sara
brooded, pulling up outside the sturdy, white-walled
cottage by the sea in which she lived most of the year.

'What a beautiful view!' murmured Suzy politely,
staring with apprehension at the vanishing horizon of
sea and sky and very little else. It was so empty! What
did Sara look at all day when Alex wasn't here?
Seagulls? Sliding out of the car, she at once felt her
ash-blonde hair begin to blow across her face in
delicate, feathery strands, and she shivered. The air
had a freshness her lungs were not accustomed to;
oxygen rushed to her head and made her dizzy.

'Yes, I love it,' Sara said blithely, unaware of her
guest's true reactions.

They found Alex downstairs when they entered the
house. Sara stiffened as the sound of Mozart floated to
her ears and she followed it, scowling crossly, into the
sitting-room where Alex was stretched out on a velvet
chaise-longue, a butter-wouldn't-melt-in-my-
mouth expression on his face as he looked round at
them.

'What are you doing? I thought I told you to stay in
bed?' Sara demanded, her face accusing.

'I wanted to be downstairs when Suzy arrived,' he

informed her, his lean face maddeningly bland. 'I'm very glad to see you, Suzy; I hope you're not going to talk to me as if I've become mentally deficient just because I picked up some stupid virus out East.'

'I'm strictly neutral,' she disclaimed at once. 'Don't ask me to take sides.'

'Ah, a conscientious objector,' drawled Alex, then held out his hand. 'Is that a present for me? Clever of you; just what I feel like reading—a good thriller.'

Suzy was bewildered for a second, then realised that he was talking about Liam's book, which she was carrying in one hand.

'Oh,' she said, flustered. 'This? I was reading it on the train and ...'

'Don't tell me how it ends,' he interrupted, his hands still impatiently gesturing. 'I've read some good reviews of this—I meant to buy it myself. It's a first book. The writer really knows his stuff; he was a racing driver himself until he was involved in a bad accident some years back.'

Suzy bit back a sigh and gave him the book, realising she had little choice. Alex was far too sharp-eyed; he might pick up hidden vibrations from her if she argued. He had no idea that she knew Liam; she had never talked about her personal life and she did not intend to start.

'Did you bring me my mail?' he asked eagerly, and she produced a large folder of letters and messages from her suitcase. Sara gave Alex a grim look and went off to the kitchen to make some tea while Suzy sank into an armchair, clutching the folder on her lap. Alex was flicking over the pages of Liam's book.

'Why don't I skim through these and give you their gist?' she suggested tactfully, but Alex shot her a dry, comprehending stare, closing the book with a snap.

'I'm quite capable of reading a few letters! Sara got at you on the way here, I suppose? Take no notice; she refuses to believe I'm almost back to normal, but I get stronger every day. I asked you down here to work, and I intend to catch up with what's been happening while I've been flat on my back, so don't give me any more nonsense.'

Suzy sighed. She could see that Alex was in a very fractious mood.

Early on Sunday morning, Suzy woke up when a seagull screamed past her window. Yawning, she lay in the narrow bed, staring at the pale dawn light filtering through the curtains, thinking about Alex and Sara. She had been rather surprised to find it easier to manage Alex than she'd expected; he had put up some resistance briefly, but his wife had firmly shepherded him back to bed after an hour of talk with Suzy and there Alex had remained for the rest of the evening. On the following day, Saturday, he had been allowed down for lunch and had spent a good deal of time excitedly talking about Liam Moor's book, without, apparently, noticing Suzy's reluctance to listen. She couldn't help a flicker of pride in the complimentary remarks Alex made about Liam's writing, even while she tried to steer the conversation into other channels.

Liam had once told her that he wanted to write; she had stored that unexpected facet of his nature away with all the other things she was learning about him three years ago. It had seemed surprising at the time; Liam was so very much a man of action, restless and full of physical energy. When he wasn't racing cars he was riding in point-to-points or climbing in the Welsh hills or merely playing tennis. He was always moving at speed, pushing his body to the limit, testing himself against other men and perhaps against his own personal best. Suzy hadn't been able to imagine him putting up with the sedentary life of a writer, shut up within four walls for hours at a time, sitting in one place in front of a typewriter. It was a contradiction of everything she knew about him, and yet when she saw those books in the railway station bookstall she hadn't been surprised. Shocked and stiff with tension, because seeing Liam's name and graphic cover picture had brought back so many memories she only wanted to forget, yet not really surprised by the realisation that Liam had written a book or that it had been published.

Whatever Liam Moor wanted, he had always managed to get—whatever the cost to other people.

Suzy sat up in bed, wincing at the thought, and swung her feet to the carpet. She needed some coffee—strong, black coffee. She must not let herself think about Liam; it had been a bad mistake to buy a copy of his book. She had known it instinctively at the time, and hesitated, but curiosity had got the better of her; now she had interested Alex in the book, which was alarming. Alex had been cooped up here for too long with very little to think about. Liam's book had distracted him which had obviously pleased his wife, but Suzy was nervous because the more Alex talked about Liam, the stronger become the likelihood that she would make some slip and give away the fact that she knew him.

Fortunately, Alex never attempted to probe into her private life, unlike her mother. Mrs Froy worried about her youngest daughter, convinced that, at twenty-five, Suzy was dangerously set on course for a lonely future. Her two older sisters had both married young and now had children; Suzy's failure to do the same made her mother fret endlessly. Suzy's career was very glamorous; Mrs Froy enjoyed boasting about 'My daughter, who's secretary to the famous film director. Alex Stevenson . . .' and showing Suzy's postcards from Los Angeles or Venice or Rio to all her friends and neighbours, but she still felt that Suzy's job was just something interesting to do until the right man came along.

But there was a lot about Suzy that her mother didn't know, and that Suzy intended she should never know.

She tiptoed downstairs into the cleverly designed modern kitchen; she didn't want to wake Sara, who must be very tired after these long weeks of nursing Alex back to health. Suzy had admired her patience yesterday. After lunch Alex had become very irritable; by the time he was back upstairs Suzy's nerves had been on edge and she could guess how Sara must have felt if he had been like that off and on ever since he came home from the hospital.

Sara had come back, grimacing at her. 'Sorry about that, but you know what men are when they're ill—

back to childhood in a flash!'

'Yes,' Suzy had agreed slowly. 'But I hadn't expected Alex to be like that.'

'No?' Sara had said, looking amused. 'Alex is pure male. To his fingertips.'

Suzy had started to laugh and Sara had joined in; from the bedroom above they heard a thud as Alex crossly dropped a book on to the floor and they had stifled their laughter in case he came back downstairs to find out what was so funny.

Suzy found herself smiling now, remembering it, as she filled the coffee percolater and got down a buttercup-yellow pottery coffee mug. Sara was right; Alex was behaving like a small child.

It was almost nine o'clock by the time she had drunk some coffee and eaten a sliver of thin toast. She decided to go and have a shower in the small bathroom on the ground floor; that way she wouldn't run the risk of waking Sara and Alex yet. Last night, Sara had told her that they always got up very late on a Sunday morning.

She was actually under the shower when she heard the doorbell ring. Startled, Suzy groped for the towel, turning off the warm water with her other hand. A towelling bathrobe hung on the door. It must be Alex's, Suzy thought; it was far too long and broad to belong to Sara. But she was in a hurry; she wanted to get to the front door before the peremptory ringing woke the two sleepers upstairs, so she pulled on the bathrobe and tied it round her waist before she ran into the hall.

There was no sound from upstairs, luckily. She

sighed in relief and pulled open the front door, holding the loose neckline of the robe together with one hand.

For what seemed an eternity she didn't believe her eyes; they stared, darkening, at the man staring back at her in just as much disbelief. It would have been hard to say which was the more incredulous.

She thought at first glance that he hadn't changed an inch; his rough, dark hair was as untidy as ever, his lean body as restlessly magnetic. Liam was a tall man, with enormous physical presence, one of those men who can't walk into a room without catching every eye, but he had always carried himself casually, wearing jeans and T-shirts most of the time, easy to talk to, wickedly funny at parties, a man people instinctively liked and could relax with, even on a first meeting.

As they stared at each other, Suzy gradually began to realise that she had been wrong on her first impression. Liam had changed. She had never seen that expression on his face before: his mouth hard with contempt, his grey eyes coldly cynical. He wasn't casually dressed, either: his smooth-fitting grey suit looked very expensive, as did the striped red and white silk shirt and dark maroon silk tie. As far as she could see, there were no physical scars from the crash three years ago, but Liam's mind carried scars which showed in the way he watched her.

Typically, he was the first to recover his self-possession. 'What are you doing here?'

Still dazed, Suzy stammered, 'I . . . I'm spending the weekend here.'

'With Stevenson?' The whiplash question made her flinch, but she lifted her chin and out-stared him.

'I'm Mr Stevenson's secretary, as it happens!' The defiance in her tone somewhat undermined the dignity she was aiming for, and she saw his mouth twist cynically.

'Oh, that's the job description these days, is it? Secretary wanted, must be prepared to work nights and weekends, salary negotiable.' He inspected her from head to toe as he spoke, his stare wandering from her angry face to her trembling hand, clutching the lapels of the robe across her naked breasts, and down from that over the slim curves of a body the damp material covered but did little to conceal.

Suzy's face burned. 'Very funny, but you're jumping to conclusions! Alex is just my boss!'

'Oh, of course,' he said, showing white teeth in a barbed smile. 'I can see you work very hard.' His eyes flickered over her again with an insolent mockery that made her want to hit him. 'I didn't realise the casting couch extended to secretarial jobs, but I suppose it's logical. I'm sure you had plenty of competition, too; a lot of girls would no doubt love to work for Alex Stevenson. He can probably pick and choose. Some of them could probably even type.'

The lazy drawl was making her want to scream. 'Your mind is disgusting!' she hissed, shaking in her efforts at self-control. If she did hit him, she suspected he'd hit her back, and his muscles made him an opponent to be wary of.

'Did I score a bullseye?' he enquired, smiling as though she had paid him a compliment, and a chill ran down her spine. He might look much the same, but this was not the man she had known—that Liam would never have made such cynical comments.

'No, you didn't,' she said through her teeth. 'You've got entirely the wrong impression, and you're lucky Alex isn't around to hear any of this!'

'I'm shaking in my shoes,' he mocked, leaning againt the door in a casual pose which conveyed as much insult as the biting words he had been flinging at her. 'Where is he, anyway? Hiding upstairs somewhere?'

'He's still in bed.' She eyed his expression angrily. How dared he look at her like that? Who did he think he was? 'With his wife!' she flung at him, seeing him stiffen with a jab of triumph.

'Wife?'

'Yes, his wife, Sara. And before you come up with any more of your insults, they're very happily married and in love with each other and Alex is nothing more than my boss. I'm here for the weekend to work because he's been ill for some time and he wants to deal with a big backlog of letters that have had to go unanswered for weeks.' She paused, but Liam seemed to have no answer to all that. His grey eyes had narrowed, flickering slightly as he thought over what she had said.

'I don't know why *you're* here,' she said, and Liam answered that brusquely.

'He rang me yesterday evening and asked me to call in here on my way back to London.'

Suzy said slowly, 'He rang you and asked you to come and see him?' Why on earth should Alex have rung him? He hadn't mentioned it; in fact, he hadn't given her any indication that he knew Liam.

'That's right.'

'He didn't tell me.'

'Does he tell you everything?' Liam was frowning again. 'How long have you worked for him?'

'A year.' She met his stare, bristling. 'And don't start jumping to conclusions again. I told you, Alex is . . .'

'I know, just your boss. Look, fascinating though it is to catch up on all your news, I'm in a hurry, so could you let him know I'm here? I've had to drive ten miles from Rye this morning, and I've gone right out of my way to call in here, at his suggestion. I'll be bloody mad if I've wasted my time. I've still got over seventy miles to do by one o'clock because I'm having lunch with someone in London.'

It was when he mentioned Rye that she realised that he must have been staying with his parents. She had never actually met them, but she remembered Liam talking about their tiny, eighteenth-century fisherman's cottage in the winding back streets of the old town on the hill above the sea. His parents had bought the house when his father retired from a job on the railways. Liam was their only child; his parents had been unable to have any more and had centred their whole lives on their son. Liam had once told Suzy that his mother hated to know he was racing and constantly pleaded with him to get out of the job. She had never watched him; she was too terrified, afraid that one day he would crash.

Of course, when he did crash, it wasn't on a race

track, but it was unlikely that the irony of that had occurred to his mother when she heard the news.

Backing into the cottage, Suzy said, 'You'd better come in, anyway. I'll wake Sara; she may know if Alex was expecting you.'

'Of course he expects me! I told you, he rang me.' He closed the front door and followed her into the sitting-room, which was shadowy because the curtains were still closed, Suzy drew them to let in the morning sunlight, acutely aware of Liam watching her.

'You know him?' she asked, turning.

'We've never met. Apparently Stevenson got in touch with my publisher, whom he does know, and it was Bill who gave him my parents' telephone number. Bill knew I was in Rye for the weekend, and in the circumstances he didn't think I'd mind talking to Stevenson.'

'Circumstances?' she repeated, her mind working overtime trying to guess why Alex wanted to talk to him. It flashed into her head suddenly: Alex must be interested in the film rights of Liam's book! That hadn't occurred to her before, but it should have done. She knew Alex was always on the look-out for suitable material to shape into film scripts. Oh, my God, she thought grimly; if I hadn't bought Liam's book, Alex might never have got around to reading it or invited Liam here today. If only she'd walked out of that bookstore without looking back! Hadn't she known it would be a mistake to buy a copy?

'Stevenson didn't mention what was on his mind?' asked Liam, and she shook her head.

'Sit down, please. I'll call Sara; I'm sure she'll be down to talk to you at once.'

As she walked towards the door, Liam caught hold of her shoulder, his hand somehow managing to drag the robe sideways, exposing her breast. She gave a little gasp, hurriedly pulling the lapels together again, her face hot.

'Why, what's the matter, Suzy?' he asked mockingly. 'You look as if you've had an electric shock.'

'You made me jump,' she said, lying in her teeth and hating the gleam in his eyes, the twist of his mouth. He knew, of course, exactly what it had done to her to have him touch her again. She had forgotten the extremity of feeling he had always been able to arouse, but he hadn't forgotten; she could see that in the way he watched her.

'I was only going to ask if Stevenson was over this mysterious illness,' he told her. 'How long will it be before he gets back to work at the studios?'

'At the moment, we've no idea—a month, perhaps less. Now, please let me call Sara.'

She tried not to run as she left the room, but she couldn't get away fast enough. She needed time to think about the consequences of her impulsive act in the railway bookstore. By buying his book she had brought Liam back into her life, and she had a sinking feeling in the pit of her stomach. She had never told Alex and Sara that she knew Liam, but there was no way that she could keep it a secret now and they were bound to be curious, ask questions, watch her with Liam and wonder why she hadn't mentioned the fact that she knew him.

As if that wasn't complicated enough, something else dawned on her—if Alex made a film of Liam's book, it would mean seeing Liam around all the time. If she knew Alex, he'd want Liam to work on the film script; that was his usual practice, to get the original writer involved if he made a novel into a film.

She had hated reading that book because of what it said about Liam's feelings for her, the depth of his contempt and hatred. How could she stand watching it being turned into a film? Watching some actress playing her, breathing life into the twisted lie which Liam had made of her character?

She stood outside Alex's bedroom door, biting her lip, nerving herself to tap on the panels. She couldn't bear it. She'd have to resign, and the sooner the better. As soon as Liam had gone, she would hand in her notice.

CHAPTER TWO

WHEN Suzy tapped at the door eventually, she heard a confused mumble and then a groan before Sara padded to the door, barefoot, opened it and looked at her blankly.

'I'm sorry to wake you up, but Alex has a visitor.'

'Not L.J.?' Sarah grimaced, and Suzy shook her head.

'Liam Moor—he says Alex rang him last night and asked him to call in here on his way to London.'

'Liam Moor?' repeated Sara, frowning. 'Who on earth . . .'

From the dimness of the bedroom behind her came an exclamation, 'My God, I'd forgotten all about him!'

Sara swung, her expression ominous. 'What have you been up to behind my back?'

Suzy didn't want to make a third at that argument, so she said quietly, 'I've put him in the sitting-room. I'm going to go and get dressed now, OK?'

Alex loomed up in his black and gold striped dressing-gown, rapidly tying the belt. 'Couldn't you make some coffee first, Suzy? I'll be down in two minutes.'

'Oh, Alex, you really are maddening!' wailed Sara and her husband dropped a light kiss on her ruffled gold-red hair.

'This isn't business, darling. This is just a casual chat. No hassle involved.'

Suzy sighed. 'I'll go and make the coffee, then.' As she turned she heard Sara ask, 'But who is this man?'

Suzy went back downstairs into the kitchen and began to make coffee. While it was percolating she ran up to her bedroom and slipped into a cream silk blouse and pleated black skirt, deliberately choosing the most demure of the three outfits she had brought down here with her. She ran a brush over her short ash-blonde hair, eyeing the brilliance of her eyes with misgiving. She looked far too excited; that was worrying. She turned from her reflection, biting her lip, and flew back to the kitchen just in time to turn off the coffee before it exploded.

She heard Alex's voice in the sitting-room as she passed the door; he sounded very friendly, but Liam's answering tone had a slightly reserved note, as though Liam was being very careful about how he replied. No doubt he was taken aback to be approached by Alex directly, since the film rights were normally bought through an agent and the writer often didn't meet the film company executives until much later. That was how Alex usually handled things, but his weeks of illness had made him hyperactive mentally, chafing at the bit as he waited to get back to work.

Suzy tapped at the door before opening it, the coffee tray balanced on her hip. Alex was lying on the sofa again, no doubt on his wife's orders. Liam was on his feet, standing beside the window. She got the impression that he had been prowling around the room while Alex talked. He swung towards her and came to take the tray out of her hands; she stiffened as she felt the slow deliberate needle of his stare move from her sleek fair head to her black shoes. His grey eyes had an icy eloquence, mocking her carefully chosen image. The demure look didn't fool him, those eyes told her, and Suzy's teeth met.

She would have left the room at once if Alex hadn't said lazily, 'Pour the coffee for us, would you, Suzy? How do you like it, Liam? Black or white? Sugar? Oh, by the way, this is my secretary, Suzy Froy. It was Suzy who brought your book to my attention; she gave it to me on Friday.'

Liam, setting the tray down on a low coffee table, straightened and looked sharply at Suzy, his brows together.

She avoided meeting his eyes, beginning to pour the coffee. Alex went on talking.

'The minute I read it, I had a hunch it would make a very interesting film—if we can get a script as good as the book, that is, and that isn't as simple as it may sound. If your agent talks to my people, we can put the business side straight first, then I'd like you to have a shot at a draft script.'

Suzy handed him his cup and he said absently, 'Thanks, Suzy,' then looked at her in surprise as she gave the other cup to Liam. 'You forgot to ask Liam if he takes sugar and cream!'

Flushing, she gave Liam a brief look. 'Sorry.'

'Black without sugar is perfect,' he said drily, knowing that she hadn't needed to ask, and knowing, too, that she was hoping to avoid having to tell Alex that they had met before.

She turned to leave the room, but Alex said, 'No, don't go, Suzy. I'd like you to sit in on this discussion. Liam has never tried his hand at scripting before and he thinks he needs some help, at least to start with. It occurred to me that Carina would be willing to give him a few tips.'

On what? Suzy thought wryly, although she fought to keep her expression blank. Carina Davis was a clever professional writer, not original by any means, yet constantly in demand to doctor the scripts of other authors whose work hadn't quite made the grade. Carina herself had never come up with anything individual enough to lift her into the top earning bracket, but she dressed and lived expensively and moved in the same circle as many of the cinema's top stars, although her name wasn't known to the general public.

Carina was also a strikingly good-looking woman with a string of male scalps on her belt. Wives became worried when they saw their husbands with her, but her affairs were brief. Brief, and spectacular. The men took years to recover.

'I'm sure Carina will be delighted,' said Suzy without looking at Liam. She knew Carina quite well by now; she knew her taste in men, and Liam would be a marked target the minute Carina laid eyes on him. Liam was attractive, with a glamorous background and an exciting potential future—Carina would gobble him up.

Alex laughed. 'From her acid tone, you can see that Suzy doesn't have much time for Carina personally—

women can never stand her. My wife hasn't two good words for her, either, but whatever she does in her private life, Carina's a professional to her fingertips; they can't deny that.'

'I wouldn't try,' said Suzy, her lip curling.

Alex eyed her. 'Hmm. What I want you to do, Suzy, is set up a meeting between Liam and Carina as soon as possible. OK?'

'Yes,' she said shortly.

'Until I'm back at work, Liam, you can keep in touch with me through Suzy. My wife insists on taking me to the Bahamas for a holiday; we'll be away for a couple of weeks, but you can always reach me via Suzy, at my office. I gather you live in London?'

'I've got a flat above a Chinese restaurant in Camden Town.'

'How very convenient. You do like Chinese food, I presume?'

'I love it, and I never have to cook a meal; I just go downstairs and eat my way through the menu. I'm becoming an expert on Cantonese cooking.'

'Carina's tastes run more to the best French cooking in the West End,' said Suzy, and Alex mocked her, grinning.

'Miaow! But she's right, Liam. Carina has no taste for anything but the best; she's an ambitious lady. Your education will be in good hands.'

Liam's grey eyes held Suzy's gaze for a second or two before she disentangled herself and looked down.

'I've had an idea,' said Alex suddenly. 'If you're driving back into London, Liam, could you give Suzy a lift? She's going back this afternoon and it would save her a tedious journey on the train.'

Suzy flushed, stiffening. 'Oh, no, I couldn't put you to any trouble ...'

'No trouble,' Liam drawled. 'I'm driving a fast car; we should get there in an hour and a half, on the motorway.'

Agitated, Suzy protested, 'Really, I'll be just as happy taking the train later today ...'

'Have you packed yet?' asked Alex, and when she shook her head quickly, hoping to plead that as an excuse, Alex said, 'Well, go and pack now, and don't take too long. Liam will have to leave in half an hour.' He stared at her as she hesitated, her face confused. 'Well, go on, Suzy! There's no time to waste.'

She went upstairs slowly, her insides churning at the prospect of spending an hour and a half alone in a car with Liam. Alex had taken her by surprise, given her no time to think of a really cast-iron excuse for turning down the drive. On the landing she met Sara, whose face was mutinous.

'I'm going in there to break things up in fifteen minutes, I don't care what Alex says,' Sara told her with decision. 'He deliberately didn't tell me that he'd invited this man; he knew what I'd say to that. I told you that if I didn't get him away from here, he'd be back at work inside a week, didn't I?'

'I don't think he will,' Suzy soothed, feeling sorry for her. Sara had been through weeks of anxiety over Alex; she was tired and looking worn out. She needed a holiday just as much as Alex did.

'Care to bet on it?' said Sara bitterly.

'He just told us that he plans to spend some weeks

in the Bahamas with you, and I think he means it,'
Suzy said, smiling, and Sara looked at her eagerly, her
face lighting up.

'Really? He said that? Oh, I hope he means it.'

'I'm sure he does.' Suzy opened the door of her
room. 'I'd better pack quickly.'

'Why the hurry? The train isn't until four.'

Sara watched her taking clothes out of the
wardrobe and chest of drawers and neatly layering
them in the open suitcase. Suzy huskily explained
without meeting her eyes.

'Mr Moor's driving me back; we'll be leaving
almost at once.'

Sara's face shone and she gave Suzy a hug. 'Oh,
thanks, Suzy, I might have known you'd come up
with something! I don't know what I'd have done
without you these last weeks. You're a tower of
strength!'

Suzy laughed wryly. 'It wasn't my idea, it was
Alex's. It will save you the drive to the station,
anyway. It's been fun this weekend; thanks for
having me here.'

'It's been a pleasure,' Sara told her with fervour,
but Suzy knew that, all the same, the other woman
would be relieved to have the cottage empty and her
husband to herself again.

Twenty minutes later, Suzy waved goodbye as
Liam's car moved off along the sunlit sea road, the
sound of the waves and the cry of the gulls
accompanying them for long after they turned inland
and struck out for London. Liam drove in silence for
some twenty minutes; they didn't look at each other,

but a tension stretched between them, quivering. When he changed gears Suzy had to fight down a sense of panic; every move he made seemed a threat.

'Want some music?' he asked abruptly, shooting her a glance. She nodded without turning her head, and Liam said, 'Well, choose a tape. They're in the glove compartment.'

She leaned forward and hunted through the assortment of tapes. 'Anything you'd like?' she asked in husky tones.

'I like them all,' he said, so she picked a tape of Spanish music.

She didn't believe this. She simply did not believe that she was sitting here in a car with Liam, driving along a busy motorway on a sunny Sunday morning, talking to him as if he were a chance-met stranger, listening to Spanish flamenco music played on a classical guitar. She began to wish she had taken a little more care when she made her choice; the rhythm of the music began to build up inside her body, her pulses were beating in time. Through her lashes she watched him, an ache in her throat.

'I'd have bet on it that you'd be married by now,' he said suddenly, and she jumped.

He turned his untidy dark head and she unguardedly looked into his eyes, her own wide, vulnerable, darkened with emotion.

'Well, I'm not.' That sounded sulky, defiant; she wished she hadn't sounded that way. She should have said calmly that marriage was no longer part of her life plan, not any more. She wanted no commitment, no involvement. She didn't want to get hurt again. A burnt child fears the fire; Suzy wouldn't even go anywhere near it again.

'But there are men in your life? Don't tell me there aren't any; I wouldn't believe that.'

'If you wouldn't believe it, there's no point in denying it, is there?' she said, hating his mocking drawl. 'Not that it's any of your business!'

'None at all,' he agreed, and for some reason that annoyed her even more.

'What about you?' she asked tightly. 'Are you married? Or going to be?'

He didn't answer for a minute or two and she held her breath, suddenly afraid he was going to tell her he was married, that there was a woman waiting for him in his London flat, perhaps even a child. A lot could happen in three years, after all. Why shouldn't he have married? In the brief silence before he spoke Suzy imagined him with another woman, marrying her, having a child; Liam part of a happy family, close and united.

'No,' he said, and the little picture evaporated like a soap bubble; Suzy breathed quietly, staring out of the window.

The Spanish music throbbed around them, too dominating to permit speech. You couldn't think, only feel, and what she felt was a physical response to the crescendo of sound. She had to keep very still not to betray it to the man sitting next to her. He seemed to have nothing more to say either, fortunately.

When he did speak she tensed at once, his voice was so hard. 'You didn't tell Stevenson that we knew each other, did you?'

'No.'

'Does he know that ...'

'He doesn't know anything about my private life, and I prefer it that way,' Suzy said roughly.

'I'm sure you do,' he drawled, and laughed, then turned his head and watched the hot colour pouring up her face. 'Mark's mother died this winter,' he told her, and she gave him a stricken look.

'Oh, I'm ...'

'Don't say you're sorry!' he interrupted harshly, and put his foot down on the accelerator so that the car shot forward, passing every other vehicle in a flash of light and noise. Suzy sat beside him rigidly; the tape ran out and the heavy beat of the music became a brooding silence.

Mark had been Liam's best friend. They had first met as eight-year-olds at a small boarding-school and had gone on to college together ten years later. Inseparable, at the same time they always were competing with each other, in both study and sport. They were instinctive competitors; it was in their natures to want to win, an inborn aggression, and although their friendship endured everything that they fought over, all the victories and defeats each snatched, they went on trying fiercely to beat each other in every possible arena. Suzy had never been able to understand what made them compete like that; she had the feeling that they couldn't have explained if she had asked them.

She thought heavily about Mark, her face pale, until Liam pulled up outside her block of flats. He insisted on carrying her case into the building; Suzy nervously unlocked her front door and turned to take it, but Liam walked past her with it and carried it into the tiny sitting-room. Suzy's flat was on the second floor; she had a kitchen just big enough to swing a cat, a bedroom twice that size and a view of treetops in some gardens nearby. The building was small enough for her to know most of the other tenants by sight and some of them quite well. Her next-door neighbour was a newcomer whom she'd only seen from a distance, but the others on the second floor had all been there when Suzy first arrived.

Liam put her case down and looked around appraisingly, while she hovered in the doorway, wondering desperately how she was going to get him to leave. She wouldn't be able to bear it if he turned that icy hostility in her direction again.

'Charming,' he drawled, his grey eyes flickering back to her. 'Did you do the décor yourself?'

She nodded, clutching the door handle, 'You'd better not leave your car parked outside for long,' she hinted.

'There were no yellow lines,' he dismissed, shrugging.

'All the same . . .'

He smiled slowly and her blood ran cold. 'You seem very edgy,' he remarked, the softness of the tone no reassurance at all. 'I don't make you nervous, do I, Suzy?'

She knew that he was threatening her even while he smiled as if it was all a joke. Lifting her chin in defiance, she shook her head.

'Of course not. Why should you?'

'Why, indeed?' He walked over to the window and pulled back an edge of the lace curtain to stare out. 'After all, it's broad daylight and we're in the middle of London; why should you be nervous?' He had his back to her now, yet she still felt his concentration on her and her pulses beat erratically at throat and wrist.

'You'll be late for your lunch appointment,' she suggested, and he laughed.

'She'll wait for me.'

Suzy drew a painful breath and Liam swung to watch her face, his eyes narrowed and gleaming. She found herself staring into them, hypnotised, unable to look away, waiting in suspension for whatever was coming. All her instincts told her that something was about to happen; Liam hadn't insisted on coming in here just to admire the view from her window. She tried to read the expression of those hard, bright eyes, to guess what was in his mind, but before she could decipher their message, Liam swerved towards her and caught hold of her arms.

'Don't!' she broke out, wincing, struggling to get away.

'Three years is a long time,' he said, as if she hadn't spoken. 'On the surface you don't seem to have altered; still the old wide-eyed, innocent look which took me in last time and no doubt fools every other man who meets you. Well, if it works, why change it. How many have there been since we last met, Suzy? Can you remember?'

She stared up at him, her eyes stretched to their limits, her skin pale, her body skaking. The bitterness in his voice pierced her; she gave a little cry of protest, and Liam's jaw hardened.

'Don't tell me there haven't been any; I wouldn't believe it. I know how passionate you are, remember.' He watched inexorably as a tide of hot colour flowed up to her hairline. 'Yes,' he whispered, 'I remember too.' He stared at her quivering mouth and to her shame she felt it part, her lips aching and heated, wanting him to kiss them. Liam bent his head suddenly and his tongue tip softly ran along the curve of her mouth, his hands moving at the same time, touching her intimately, caressingly: the soft flesh of her breasts, her slim back, her hips and buttocks, exploring the curve of her body with the same taunting insolence with which his tongue traced her lips.

In spite of her knowing the contempt he felt as he touched her, Suzy's whole body came alive under his fingers, responding with electric excitement, her skin sharply sensitive to the slide of those cool, wandering hands, the taste of his tongue. She felt her lids come down, her spine arch, her breathing hectic; Liam's mouth closed over hers and they kissed.

Then he lifted his head and laughed. 'As I suspected,' he whispered, 'I could still have you—if I wanted you.' He watched her face stiffen and burn, smiling at her, deliberately insulting her. 'But you see, I don't.'

Suzy was frozen on the spot. She felt him push her away, heard him turn and walk out of the flat, slam the front door, and knew that that was how he had planned it all along. He had carried her suitcase in here to give himself the opportunity of humiliating her; he had sat in the car next to her, all the way from Kent, working out his strategy, and he had enjoyed every second of it; his smile had made that obvious.

Her instincts had warned her, picked up what was in his mind; why had she still let him do it to her? She bit her lip, raging helplessly against herself, against Liam, her ears drumming with hurt and anger.

'Bastard,' she muttered hoarsely, wishing she had said that to him. 'Bastard!' She shouldn't have let Alex railroad her into accepting a lift from Liam; she shouldn't have let Liam come here. She had been weak and he had taken advantage of that. Men always did; why hadn't she remembered that? It was typical, too, that he blamed her for everything that had happened; he felt none of the guilt he had offloaded on to her. It was all her fault. Men had been getting away with that hoary old excuse for centuries—since the Garden of Eden, in fact, when Adam turned round and told his accusing God, 'The woman tempted me . . .' That was how Liam saw it, too, and Suzy hated him for that.

CHAPTER THREE

SUZY brooded all evening over what to do next, tempted to ring Alex at once and tell him she must resign yet feeling unable to do that while Alex was still recovering from the effects of his illness. She knew it would probably bring him hurrying back to London, in spite of all Sara's protests, because there had to be someone in his office whom he could trust to cope with the day-to-day routine as well as any emergencies that might crop up. Alex certainly wouldn't go to the Bahamas, and if Suzy caused a recurrence of his illness she would blame herself. Sara would blame her too, especially as she knew she would never be able to tell either of them the truth, the real reason for her sudden wish to leave.

Would Liam say anything? she wondered, her face distraught. She was sure he wouldn't because, in spite of his refusal to take any of the blame, he must know he did share some of the responsibility. He wouldn't want to talk about it any more than she did. Guilt was corrosive, ate into the very fabric of your mind. You couldn't simply shed it; you had to accept what you had caused and learn to live with it, however painful.

For the moment, for Alex's sake, she would have to put up with dealing with Liam, but she determined fiercely to do so at a distance, by phone. She would take care never to set eyes on him again.

On the Monday morning she rang Carina Davis. The soft purr of the other woman's voice changed when she realised who was speaking.

'Oh, hello, what can I do for you.' Carina's natural tone was brisk and efficient, but when a man was in earshot her manner became meltingly female, a little too obviously.

'Alex asked me to ring you,' said Suzy, and went on to explain why she had been told to get in touch with Carina.

'Liam Moor? Of course I know who he is! I've seen him race and I've just been reading this book. I'd simply love to work with him, tell Alex. How is darling Alex, by the way?'

'Much better.'

'Super,' Carina said indifferently. 'Look, give me Liam Moor's telephone number and I'll call him and make a date. No need for you to arrange it; I'll deal with him.'

'Thank you,' said Suzy, her voice expressionless although her face was screwed up with dislike and resentment. She gave Carina Liam's number and rang off. No doubt they would get on like a house on fire; Carina would give him doe-eyed smiles and flatter him outrageously and he would love it. Suzy picked up a pencil and held it tightly as she hunted for the number of the studio rights department. She had to let them know that Alex wanted to acquire the rights of Liam's book and they were not going to be very happy when they heard that Alex had already approached him.

What did it matter to her if Liam dated someone

else? He hated her; she ought to hate him. She kept trying to convince herself she did, but deep inside her ran that other emotion, the wild feeling which had surfaced when he kissed her. He had tormented her with her own feelings, mocking her helpless self-betrayal.

The pencil broke in her fingers and she jumped at the sharp little crack of sound, dropping the two broken halves on her desk.

'You look like a thundercloud,' a voice said, and she started, looking quickly at the door.

'Oh, hello, Joshua.' She managed a smile; it wasn't very convincing and the broad, fair young man in the doorway studied her thoughtfully.

'You look as though you've had a bad weekend. Of course!' He snapped finger and thumb dramatically, coming over to perch on her desk. 'You went to see Alex, didn't you? Was he raging like a caged lion? Eating furniture, chewing carpets. These creative types are all the same.' He peered into her face. 'I see shadows under those baby blue eyes, but don't worry—I know exactly what you need. Lunch, a bottle of wine and a heavy dose of sweet talk across a table at El Sombrero!'

She laughed, shaking her head. 'Idiot!'

'I didn't hear that. One o'clock downstairs?'

'Joshua, it's a kind thought, but ...'

He put a large hand over her mouth. 'Don't say but. Say yes. I need cheering up, too. We'll solace each other.'

Over his hand, she looked at him searchingly and Joshua grinned with a wry self-derision.

'Yes, Linda flew to Spain this morning, dripping with cameras and totally oblivious of the broken heart she left behind her. I must be a masochist. You'd think that by now I'd realise I was wasting my time, wouldn't you? She's another of these creative types: obsessed with her work and blind to everything else. They start shooting the film next week—a fifty-day schedule, which means Linda won't be back for a couple of months. I feel a fool, trying to compete with a bloody camera.'

'I can't advise you, Joshua,' Suzy said gently. 'I'm no good at coping with my own love life.'

'I didn't know you had one,' he said, staring.

'Thanks!'

Her flush made him grimace apologetically. 'Sorry, I didn't mean to sound insulting. It's just that you're such a secretive little mouse, you don't give a thing away. Is it anyone I know? I thought it was the terrible trauma of working for Alex that put those shadows under your eyes.' Then his face stiffened, his eyes widened. 'It isn't ...?'

She looked back at him, puzzled, then the thought leapt from his mind to hers and she laughed angrily. 'No, Joshua, it is not Alex! My God, I'm not that crazy!'

'I never thought it was for a second,' Joshua lied, a little pink around the ears. He was almost thirty but looked younger, partly because of his fair colouring and partly because he had a cheerful, irrepressible manner. He found his job in the accounts department of Empire Films extremely dull and limited, but he stayed because he got a kick out of glimpsing the more glamorous figures who flitted in and out of the building all the time. Joshua had no creative spark himself, but admired it in others, which might explain his passion for Linda Black. Linda had come the tough route to the top, starting as a stills photographer's assistant and somehow climbing steadily from job to job until at twenty-nine she was an assistant director. She had all the flair and originality Joshua lacked, and Suzy often wondered why Linda didn't make it clear to Joshua that he was wasting his time. The fact that she didn't, that he kept hovering around her and she didn't seem able to end their relationship, probably meant that for some reason Linda liked him more than she was ready to admit, but in the mean time it was Joshua who was getting hurt, and Suzy felt very sorry for him.

'Lunch?' he asked a little pleadingly, and she sighed, unable to turn him down. He was probably right, anyway; they both needed to forget their problems and lunch at a good restaurant would be fun.

'OK. Thank you, Joshua.'

He grinned and made his way to the door. 'One o'clock, then, by the main entrance.'

Suzy picked up the phone after he had vanished, and rang the rights department, who made the sort of irritable fuss she had expected. Alex shouldn't have spoken to the author directly; he should have let them deal with the negotiations before he approached the man. Now they would have their hands tied behind their backs. The author and his agent would know Alex wanted the book badly; that would put the price up. Really, Mr Stevenson ought to know better!

'I'm sorry, I know you're right, but I can't control Mr Stevenson,' Suzy said wearily when the man on the other end of the phone stopped complaining.

'I don't know what Mr Jonas is going to say,' the voice threatened.

'Well, Mr Jonas will be back this week. You can give him your point of view yourself. In the mean time, perhaps you'd like to start the negotiations moving?' Suzy was sympathetic to the other man's problem, but she was in no mood to listen to much more of this. After all, she was only Alex's secretary and obviously had had nothing to do with the way Alex handled his approach to Liam, but then she was often held responsible for what her boss did, especially, oddly enough, by other secretaries. They seemed to believe that a secretary secretly pulled the strings which opened her boss's mouth or made him move. Suzy had decided long ago that either their bosses were much more malleable than her own, or that the other girls were suffering from a common delusion.

Having dealt with the rights department, she tackled the pile of letters waiting for attention. None of them was urgent; she had taken all those down to Kent that weekend. These were the run-of-the-mill stuff, mostly needing a standard reply, the form of which was already on her computer which did the work for her by printing each out with a different name each time. Suzy signed them with a rubber stamp of Alex's signature. It looked amazingly genuine, and she had got through the whole pile by lunchtime.

Lunchtime with Joshua was rather fun. The food was Mexican and the wine cheap and drinkable. Joshua insisted on ordering another bottle after rapidly finishing the first, and was soon in a very good mood indeed. He sang off key to the intrusive tape of sweet, romantic music playing over the loudspeaker near their table, which earned them some irritable looks from other customers, so Suzy good-humouredly guided him back to the office as soon as he had had several black coffees. By then Joshua had become melancholy; he wouldn't be parted from her at his own floor in the block but stayed in the lift and came with her to her office talking gloomily about Linda's coldness and his own misery.

Suzy sat him in a chair and went to make some strong coffee. By then Joshua had begun to sing a very sad song. People down the corridor stuck their heads out of their doors and asked, 'Who brought a dog in here?'

Suzy forced Joshua to take the mug of coffee. He sipped it, then leaned his head against her waist, saying, 'You wouldn't treat a man like that, would you, Suzy? You're a nice girl. Why don't I fall in love with you?'

She ruffled his hair lightly. 'Come on, Joshua, you've got to do some work today, you know.'

A movement near the door caught her attention; she looked sideways and was shaken to see Liam watching them, his grey eyes glacial.

'Sorry to interrupt,' he said, showing his teeth in a

smile which was no smile at all.

Joshua swayed backwards, gazing at him owlishly. 'Who's that?' he asked Suzy. 'I don't know him.'

Liam's brows lifted. 'Is he drunk?'

'Who's drunk?' demanded Joshua, getting up and stumbling almost at once. 'Say that again.'

'Sit down, Joshua,' Suzy said quietly, wishing the earth would open up and swallow them both. The disdainful expression with which Liam watched Joshua made her wince. She took hold of Joshua's arms and pushed him back on to his chair, giving him his black coffee again. 'Drink all of this and be quiet,' she told him, before looking at Liam as calmly as she could. 'Will you come into Mr Stevenson's office for a moment.' She led the way, conscious of him treading close behind her, sending shivers down her spine.

Liam closed the door and leaned on it, his long, lean body casually relaxed. He was wearing charcoal-grey trousers and a heavy cream wool fisherman's sweater under a black leather jacket; he looked far less formidable in them than he had in the expensively tailored suit he wore in Kent, but Suzy found it just as hard to keep her cool as he watched her.

'When the cat's away the mice will play?' he asked with dry distaste. 'If Stevenson gets to hear you've been having these little parties for two up here, you may have trouble keeping your job.'

She took a deep breath and counted to ten; he wasn't getting her to lose her temper, not this time.

'I've talked to Carina Davis and she'll be in touch with you very soon, Mr Moor,' she said politely.

'She already has; we have a lunch date for

Wednesday,' he informed her. She wasn't very surprised at the speed with which Carina had moved—trust her to move fast, where an attractive man was concerned, she thought—but she was at a loss to know why Liam was here, in that case.

Her blue eyes regarded him with bewilderment, and Liam said softly, 'I shall want you to be there.'

Suzy was appalled, her face reflecting as much. 'Me? But ... why?'

'Stevenson wants you to act as liaison between me and Miss Davis,' he said in a silky voice, his smile very reasonable and totally untrustworthy.

She shook her head quickly. 'Oh, no, you've got that wrong—he said I would act as a liaison between you and him, while he's in the Bahamas and out of touch.'

'I've talked to him on the phone this morning and he agrees that it would be valuable for you to sit in on my first discussion with Miss Davis,' Liam countered. 'After all, she and I have never met. It will smooth the way if you're there.'

She swallowed, as nervous as a kitten at the prospect of making an uneasy third at that meeting. Carina wouldn't be pleased either; in fact, she would be furious. The company of her own sex was not something she sought and, when a man was involved, was more often something she strenuously avoided.

From the other office Joshua raised his voice plaintively. 'Suzy, where did you go? Come back, I need you.'

Liam regarded her with narrowed, gleaming eyes. 'He needs you,' he repeated. 'Does he get you?'

Suzy walked over to Alex's large, immaculately tidy desk, and picked up a notepad. The desk was tidy because Alex was away and she could keep it clear; when he was here he liked it awash with paper. That made him feel busy.

'This lunch on Wednesday,' she said, pencil poised. 'Where and at what time?'

'The Savoy at twelve-thirty,' he said, and she did a double-take.

'The Savoy?'

'Miss Davis suggested it,' he murmured, his mouth crooked with amusement. 'She has expensive tastes, I gather; she seemed to assume I did too. You should have told her that my taste ran in quite another direction.' His eyes were wandering over her insolently and she kept her eyes on the pad as she wrote down the time and place of the lunch, trying not to betray her awareness of that stare.

'I don't have that sort of conversation with Miss Davis,' she told him flatly.

Joshua was crooning in the far room. 'Suzy, Suzy, Suzy!'

Liam straightened the elegant curve of his body as if he was leaving, and turned to face the door. Suzy moved towards him to follow him out, but he suddenly swung to face her, the mockery gone from his eyes and his mouth a hard line.

'What do you see in that guy? Why pick someone like that?' He suddenly caught her face between his hands, his palms against her forehead, crushing inwards with a force that made her cry out.

'You're hurting!'

'Am I?' He tilted her head backwards and stared down insistently into her face. 'I wish I knew what went on inside this head of yours. Why do you always pick weak men? Are you afraid of strong ones? Scared of what they might want from you? Men like that guy in there, men like Mark, don't make too many demands, do they?'

The name hit her and she turned white and stiffened, the sound echoing in her ears, inside her brain.

He watched her remorselessly, refusing to let her hide a thing from him and Suzy trembled in sudden anger. She didn't want a confrontation with him; it was the very last thing she wanted. It couldn't do any good, it would only tear her apart and hurt him, but Liam kept trying to force it on her and sooner or later she was going to have to face the accusation in those icy grey eyes.

She jerked her head backwards, pushing at his shoulders at the same time, and broke free.

'*I* didn't kill Mark!' she said huskily, and saw his face tighten and grow deathly white.

She pushed past him, opened the door and went into the other office where Joshua hailed her delightedly.

'Where did you get to.'

Liam crossed the office in a few long strides and vanished, slamming the door behind him. Joshua's head swivelled round and he stared, bolt-eyed. 'What was that?'

'A thunderstorm,' Suzy said with dry lips. She hadn't wanted to hurt Liam, but he had left her no choice. 'Look, we've got to sober you up and get you back to work before you get fired,' she told Joshua. 'I'll get you some more black coffee, then you must go.'

She wanted Joshua to go and leave her alone. She had a headache; the back of her head was throbbing violently as if a little man with a hammer was beating on it. As she watched Joshua drinking coffee she wasn't seeing him at all; she was inwardly seeing Liam's face whiten and grow rigid as she had said; '*I* didn't kill Mark!' It had been cruel. She wished she could take it back; she wished she hadn't said it. Liam had provoked her into blurting it out, and it was the truth; that was the most unforgivable thing about it. It was the truth and Liam knew it. He would hate her even more now.

Joshua departed to face the head of his department and Suzy settled down to finish her day's work. While Alex was away, it wasn't onerous, since most people had heard that he was on sick leave and had given up ringing him, and without Alex to create turmoil around her, Suzy had managed to put the office into better shape than it had been. The files were up to date and tidy, the paperwork had been dealt with, and Suzy could get through the routine work in a few hours at the moment. She could have gone home after lunch, but she stayed at the desk, trying to distract herself with tedium.

At five-fifteen, just as she was thinking of leaving, the phone rang. Suzy sighed, picking it up reluctantly. 'Hello? Mr Stevenson's office.'

'Suzy?' an agitated voice asked. 'Look, I know it's

short notice and I wouldn't ask if I wasn't absolutely desperate, but my usual girl has suddenly developed spots and her mother just rang to say she shouldn't really come in case she passed on something horrific. God knows what she's picked up, it could be chickenpox, but it leaves me in a terrible fix because Derek has to be at this dinner party. The Chairman's never invited us before and we've simply got to be there or it could mean curtains for Derek's chances of promotion this year ...'

'What time do you want me?' asked Suzy, stemming the flow as the speaker took her first real breath. She had identified her sister Clarrie during the first breathless words. The domestic crisis was typical of Clarrie, whose best-laid plans were always likely to go wrong. A malign fate had dogged Clarrie's footsteps for most of her life—she claimed it had begun the day Suzy was born and Clarissa, aged seven, stared down into the new baby's cot and cried shrilly, 'Take it back!' Her parents had declined, however, to do anything of the kind, and Clarrie felt her misfortunes had begun at that moment.

'Oh, thanks, Suzy,' Clarrie said gratefully. 'Could you make it by seven? We're supposed to be there by seven-thirty, although heaven only knows how I'm going to be ready. I haven't even bathed the baby yet, let alone myself, and the dog's run off in the direction of the golf course; he'll come back covered in mud and sand and I'll have to bath him too, before I can get ready. I hope you haven't got to cancel anything? Is there anyone at the moment? What happened to the one with the ears?'

'I can get there by seven, don't worry, and I'll deal with the dog if he isn't back soon,' Suzy said, sorting out the problems in order of importance. 'And I don't have to cancel a date. I don't know who on earth you mean by the one with ears—all my men have had ears, to my recollection.'

'Not as big as these, I hope,' said Carrie. 'William, don't hit your brother with that, you'll break it. Oh, you naughty boy, what did I tell you?' She paused briefly, Suzy heard a slap and a wail, then Clarrie reappeared briefly to say, 'Thanks, Suzy, you're an angel. See you; I've got to get the dustpan and brush.'

Suzy replaced the telephone, her expression distinctly apprehensive. Looking after her nephews at any time was a tiring chore because they were normally as slippery as eels and as charged with energy as an electric cable, but when they were in one of their hyperactive states it left you feeling like an old rag at the end of the day. The easiest member of the Coram family was, in fact, the baby, little Anna, aged seven months. Fed and dry, she happily slept for hours without making a sound.

Suzy had a feeling she had a busy evening ahead of her; drinks of water, bedtime stories and cries of 'Auntie Suzy, William hit me!' from the minute the front door closed behind Clarrie and Derek to the minute they let themselves back into the house.

When she reached her sister's house in West London she found Derek in the hall with his eyes on his watch.

'I'm sorry, am I late?' she asked, startled, and her brother-in-law gave her a wry shake of the head.

'No, Clarrie is! Clarrie!' His shout made Suzy jump and two small heads appeared over the banisters.

'Hello, Auntie Suzy. Anna's teething and Mummy can't get her to sleep,' William announced with satisfaction above the fretful crying in one of the bedrooms.

'Clarrie, we must leave *now!*' shouted Derek, and Clarrie shot to the top of the stairs, her finger to her lips.

'I've almost got her off, stop shouting!'

'You go, Clarrie, I'll take over,' Suzy soothed.

Four-year-old Derry threw himself at his mother as she began to come downstairs and clasped her leg, begging her not to go.

Suzy picked him up and promised her sister she would read him a bedtime story after she had got Anna off to sleep. Derry roared, bright red with rage and tears, Anna screamed upstairs, William decided it was an opportune moment to slide down the stairs on his bottom. Derek took his distracted wife's arm and hustled her out of the front door, issuing instructions as she went.

'Teething jelly in the cabinet in the bathroom . . . a feed at ten-thirty if we aren't back by then and she wakes up, but . . .'

'Don't wake her specially—I know, I've been through this twice before, remember, with the boys.'

'Derry, don't cry, Mummy will be home soon,' Clarrie reassured him, kissing the small, screwed-up damp face.

Derek jerked her ruthlessly out of sight and Suzy

shut the door, saying brightly to the boys, 'Now, what shall we do? Shall we go back to bed and have a bedtime story?' Although how on earth they were going to hear any of it above the baby's yelling she did not know. She headed for the stairs, carrying Derry, kicking and sobbing, dragging William with her and trying to stop him taking off his pyjamas with the spacemen on them. At the top of the stairs William wriggled free and ran into the baby's room, popping up beside her cot and shouting, '*Boo!*' with such a yell that the baby was utterly silenced. Before she began to cry again William capered about pulling funny faces and Anna hiccuped into fascinated smiles. Suzy put Derry back to bed, tucked him in, and went to collect William. She found that Anna's eyes were shut—she was sleeping the sleep of the exhausted—and William was climbing on to the windowsill to peer out at the street lamps.

Suzy grabbed him back to safety and took him to the room he shared wth his brother. By then, Derry was out of bed and playing on the floor with his wooden soldiers. Suzy put both of them into bed and told them a long story before putting out the light and going downstairs very quietly.

She sank into an armchair and looked at the clock; it was seven-thirty. She had another three hours of this, at the very least. She looked at the television set; should she get up and switch it on? She had no sooner thought that than the first wail came; it was the baby. By the time Suzy got upstairs, the two boys were out of bed again.

It was going to be a long, long evening. Suzy

thought wistfully of her own small, quiet flat. Small, quiet, *empty* flat, she expanded as she picked up the screaming baby and went in search of teething jelly. The two small boys went with her. Anything was better than going to sleep.

At ten o'clock Suzy was downstairs listening to the silence and praying it wouldn't be broken yet again. She was afraid to relax; at any minute the baby might remember her ten o'clock feed and start clamouring for that. Leaning her head back against the cushion of the armchair, Suzy let her lids descend; it was restful just to sit there. How on earth did Clarrie stay sane? It was OK for Derek, leaving every morning for work after breakfast and coming home again at six after a peaceful day at the office. Clarrie had to stay within these four walls, chained like a galley-slave to her three offspring.

Suzy thought grimly of what she would say to her mother next time Mrs Froy started urging her to get married. Just three hours of Clarrie's children and she was ready to take a week's holiday. What must it be like for Clarrie, who got precious little time off? Giving a yawn, she thought of opening her eyes to look at the clock, but didn't have the strength. Within minutes she was asleep.

'Suzy! Suzy, wake up ...'

The voice broke through the terrible sounds: crashing and splintering of metal and glass, screams, the scream of tyres, the explosion and the roar of orange flames leaping up. Suzy surfaced, white and dazed, her body as heavy as if she had been dragged

from drowning, and stared into her sister's face with
dilated eyes.

'Clarrie?' For a moment she didn't know where she
was or what had happened.

'You were having a nightmare,' Clarrie told her,
anxiously watching her. She sat down on the edge of
the chair and put an arm around her. 'My God, it
sounded terrible!'

Derek was standing by the door. He looked uneasy.
'I'll put the kettle on,' he offered, and disappeared.

Suzy discovered she was shaking and tried to stop.
The pictures were fading back into her unconscious,
safely bottled up again. She had had the dream at
frequent intervals at first: every night for weeks, and
then gradually decreasing until it stopped altogether.
Even grief has its fixed season and doesn't continue at
the same unbearable pitch; the mind can't sustain it,
it would end in madness. It must have been seeing
Liam again that opened the door and let the dream
loose; she might have expected that, if she hadn't
wanted to forget that she had ever had bad dreams at
all.

'I thought you'd got over it,' said Clarrie, and Suzy
bit down on her lower lip. So had she; she had been
too sure that it was all in the past to be careful. If she
had realised how frail her peace of mind really was she
wouldn't have bought Liam's book.

'What did I say?' she asked bleakly. The thought of
anyone listening to her when she didn't know what
she was saying appalled her.

'You were calling to Mark,' Clarrie said, and Suzy
knew instantly what that meant. It was always part of

the dream, the car turning over and over, bursting into flame and herself screaming, 'No, Mark, no!'

White-faced, she stumbled to her feet and looked blindly at the clock. 'What's the time?'

'Five past eleven,' said Clarrie automatically. 'Suzy, it's so long now—what, nearly three years? No, it was March, wasn't it? I remember how raw the weather was ...'

Suzy remembered too: the winds cruel and the sky livid and ominous. She moved to the door, trying to escape Clarrie's relentless, loving anxiety, but her sister followed, catching at her arm.

'Suzy, do you often dream like that? I thought you'd forgotten it all, you ought to have done by now. Stand still, I'm worried about you. I know Mark's death was a terrible shock, but it was always on the cards—racing drivers take those risks every day; you knew that when you got engaged to him. You can't go on mourning him for ever; you're too young to live in the past. What are you trying to do to yourself?'

'I haven't dreamt about it for months,' Suzy said shortly. 'It's late, Clarrie, and I'm very tired. I must hurry, I can get the last train with luck.'

'Don't be silly, Derek's driving you home—you know it isn't safe on the underground at this hour.' Clarrie was distracted by this practical matter and called her husband from the kitchen. 'Derek! You're driving Suzy back, aren't you?'

'Of course!' he said. 'But what about this tea I've made? Have some before you go, Suzy.'

'I'm sorry, I'm in a hurry,' she apologised.

'I hope you're not exhausted by looking after the

kids,' Derek said wryly. 'I know they can be monsters.'

'Of course not, they were angels,' Suzy lied, and he gave her a shrewd, teasing smile.

'That I don't believe, but thanks for coming to the rescue. It was a vital dinner party, I won't say we enjoyed it, because the Chairman and his wife aren't sparkling conversationalists, but it seemed to go quite well.'

Suzy grabbed her coat and Derek helped her into it instinctively. His wife was making cross faces at him behind Suzy's back, but Suzy was well aware of that, even though she didn't look.

'Stay the night, Suzy, the spare room's ready,' urged Clarrie, wanting to have a further chance to give her good advice, but Suzy wouldn't be prodded into staying. She went home and was in bed by midnight. She didn't dream at all, or if she did she didn't remember it in the morning, but the face she saw in the mirror as she put on her make-up had all the colour and vivacity of old paper.

CHAPTER FOUR

IT WAS a cold, rainy day the following Wednesday. When Suzy uncertainly walked into the main foyer of the Savoy Hotel she found a fire burning in the great hearth and a number of guests clustered on the deep sofas in front of it, enjoying the warmth after the inhospitable London streets outside. Suzy wasn't quite sure where to go and hovered, looking around her. The hotel was enormous. A liveried page came over to her and asked if he could help her.

'Miss Davis?' he smiled, when she told him who she was having lunch with. 'Of course, she's in the bar next to the River Room Restaurant.' He gave Suzy directions and she found Carina a moment later, sitting alone at a table drinking a cocktail. Suzy paused, observing her before Carina was aware of her presence, feeling a surge of insecurity about her own looks, Carina's glossy sophistication was almost an attack; she dominated everyone around her even when she ignored them. A black mink hat was perched on her swept-up black hair; her flame-coloured dress was clinging jersey wool, outlining every curve of her body. Around her neck she wore a heavy, barbaric torque of twisted gold and, in her ears, wide gold rings. Her features would have been stunning if she hadn't been wearing make-up at all, but her expertise with the brush had gilded the lily, giving her skin an enamelled perfection, flawless and smooth. Her lids were tinted with delicate purple, her mouth had the rich fullness of a persimmon.

Suzy saw all the men in the bar staring, openly or furtively, Carina lifted her glass and eyed the cloudy orange liquid without tasting it, apparently unaware of being watched.

Reluctantly, Suzy walked towards the table, feeling very pale and insignificant. Her own colouring was mute, by comparison; her ash-blonde hair and light blue eyes lacked Carina's dramatic impact; her grey and pink striped tailored dress hardly did much to draw the eye. She had never wanted to make men stare, though; she liked life peaceful and was unnerved by competition, perhaps because she was the youngest of her family and had never dared to compete with her sisters, Emily and Clarissa. Suzy's main object as a child had been to get by without trouble from all the adults in the house, and that instinct had remained with her since she became an adult herself.

Carina's head swung round as Suzy reached her, but the smile abruptly vanished when she realised it wasn't Liam joining her.

'What are you doing here? Where's Liam? Don't tell me he isn't coming!'

'As far as I know he is,' Suzy said flatly. 'Alex asked me to sit in on your first discussion, though.' She sat down, and Carina looked at her with discontent.

'Why on earth should he think that was necessary?

I don't need your help to deal with a man like Liam Moor.'

Maybe Alex had thought that Liam needed help to deal with Carina, thought Suzy, but carefully didn't say so.

'I imagine Alex wants a first-hand report of how your talks went,' she said tactfully.

'I could have given him that.' Carina's red mouth indented, then suddenly widened into a welcoming smile.

Suzy didn't need to look round to know that Liam was walking towards them. If she hadn't seen Carina's face, she would have felt his presence from the sudden bristling of every tiny hair on the back of her neck.

'You're Liam,' said Carina, holding out both hands. 'Hello, wonderful to meet you in person at last; I've been cheering you from the grandstand for years, It was a real thrill to read your book and an even bigger one when I heard we were going to work together.'

Liam's voice was deep and lazy; Suzy didn't look up to see if his face matched the charm of the tone. Instead, she studied the cocktail menu and decided to have a Manhattan.

'I'm a rank novice, you'll have to be patient with me,' Liam was saying the next time she listened in on their chat. 'You're going to have to teach me from scratch.'

'Oh, I don't believe that for an instant,' Carina

crooned. 'But I'll be happy to teach you everything I know.'

And she isn't kidding, Suzy thought, shooting a look through her lashes and intercepting the smiles they exchanged. Liam was sitting on the velvet sofa next to Carina, her leg was pressed against his and she was gazing into his eyes.

Lesson one, Suzy registered, and it has nothing whatever to do with writing a film script. She watched Carina's hand lightly brush Liam's knee: not too obviously and only for a second. Carina sipped her drink while Liam and Suzy ordered theirs, so far Liam hadn't said a syllable to Suzy and Carina was happy to follow his example. While Suzy ran her eye over the restaurant menu Carina talked about the difficulties of transferring a novel to film, the necessity for economy in dialogue.

'A film script looks very sparse, darling,' Carina said, 'but every word tells. Take that scene in your book where the hero sees the girl just before the race. You had three pages of his thoughts and their tiny conversation. On film that will melt down to an exchange of looks and maybe four words of dialogue, but it will tell everything we need to tell.'

'Shouldn't we order?' queried Suzy, speaking for the first time and indicating the waiter hovering with scarcely disguised impatience nearby.

Carina looked at the man idly. 'Oh, yes—my usual, please, just melon and sole, grilled, no vegetables, just a green salad.'

Suzy had been reading the menu greedily, dying to

test almost anything on that list, but she sighed and said she would have the same. If Carina couldn't eat rich, delicious food, neither could she.

It was over the table by the window in the River Room, as they ate their sole, that Carina said to Liam, 'The characters are beautifully defined, we don't need to alter any of them. The girl's an absolute bitch, of coure. I've met them, those cool little teases who enjoy keeping several men on a string, playing them off against each other. They're always the demure ones; butter wouldn't melt in their mouths, or so they'd love you to believe—but watch out for the claws. Under their sweet smiles they're the biggest pussycats of them all.'

Suzy felt Liam glancing sideways, his grey eyes glinting and cool. 'What do you think, Miss Froy?' he asked softly.

Suzy's jawline was rigid with tension, but she managed a tight little smile. 'I'd better not venture an opinion, Mr Moor. I've started reading the book, but I haven't finished it yet.'

'How could you bear to put it down?' Carina said at once, all enthusiasm. 'I simply read it at one sitting, and that was before Alex asked me to work with you, Liam. I loved every word; quite un-put-downable. The best thriller of the year—a straight novel, really; it's too good just to be a thriller.'

'I like thrillers, actually,' Liam said mildly, and Carina rushed to agree, nodding. 'Oh, so do I ... absolutely, but ...'

Suzy stopped listening again, wishing she was

somewhere else. She knew now why Liam wanted her to be present; he had enjoyed watching her wince over Carina's comments on the girl in his book, the girl Suzy knew was based on herself. Of course, Carina didn't know that. Nobody was likely to guess, because nobody had known about her and Mark, except Liam—but that was small comfort.

She watched the waiter whisk away her barely touched plate. 'Not hungry, Miss Froy?' mocked Liam, pretending to be concerned, and Suzy shook her head. The others chose their desert while she stared through the trees at the river.

She wished fiercely that she had not bought the copy of his book on her way down to see Alex and Sara. Every action is followed by reaction, she thought with an angry humour. Every cause has an effect.

If she hadn't gone to Brands Hatch one summer day with a young man fom her office she would never have met Mark Culloch. Suzy had been working for a City of London broker at that time and one of the stockbrokers had pursued her eagerly for weeks until she agreed to a date with him. They had driven into Kent to spend a day at the famous racing track. The young stockbroker knew Mark and insisted on taking her to meet him. He was trying to impress her; it didn't enter his head that Mark might take her away from him.

Suzy had been dazzled by Mark's good looks. He had sunny blond hair and a lot of charm. When he was relaxed and among friends, he was a lively companion, always smiling, but as she got to know him better Suzy began to recognise the signs of a split personality. Mark had a sudden, explosive temper. In that mood, he became quite irrational, and she came to recognise the tell-tale little signals of an impending explosion—rigid muscles in his face and neck, dilating pupils, a sudden snarl in his voice.

After that first meeting at Brands Hatch, Mark had invited Suzy and her date to a party that evening, and he'd contrived to get her alone and make a date to meet again next day.

'Don't tell anyone,' he had warned. 'The press would make your life hell—the gossip columns will be full of it. Let's keep this very private.'

Head spinning, she eagerly agreed, and she hadn't been surprised by the request. After all, Mark was famous, a hero to many people, one of the most brilliant of the younger racing drivers and good copy to the journalists thronging the race tracks, especially when Liam drove in the same races. Their permanent duel was famous. They encouraged the myth of their rivalry, laughing over it in private, yet it was a very real battle between them all the same. Each loved to win, but Suzy came to suspect that Mark was the more intense about it. Liam wasn't so easy to read.

Suzy never went out with the stockbroker again. She left his firm and got a job with an agency which left her plenty of spare time to see Mark.

By then she had discovered the real reason for Mark's desire for secrecy—his mother. Mrs Culloch was passionately possessive about her only son. A widow of forty-five, she had centred her whole life around Mark, adoring the limelight which surrounded him, the fame and glamour of his life. Whenever Mark raced, she was there to watch him and he was afraid of arousing her jealousy, so Suzy only saw Mark in places where word would not get back to his mother. They drove into the country, had lunch at out-of-the-way places, met at Liam's little cottage in Sevenoaks.

Liam, of coure, was in the secret, of necessity, and eventually Suzy told her sister Clarissa, because she needed to talk to someone and was afraid to confide in her parents in case they told anyone else. Mark was talking of getting married one day, by then, but their engagement, like their meetings, was totally secret.

If Mark's mother was with him Suzy found herself left with Liam. He was the smokescreen Mark threw up to deceive his mother. 'I know I can trust him to keep his hands to himself,' Mark told Suzy cheerfully. 'He's a wicked philanderer, but the one girl he wouldn't steal is mine. Liam and I go too far back.'

'But if your mother thinks I'm dating Liam, what will she say when we tell her the truth?' Suzy had asked him anxiously, and Mark had shrugged.

'We'll cross that bridge when we come to it.' Mark had been hiding things from his mother for years, and Liam had been helping him do it, because Mrs Culloch's love was smothering and claustrophobic; she couldn't bear Mark to stray too far from her side and was jealous of everyone of her own sex who came too close to him.

'Liam will pick you up and bring you to the party,' Mark would tell Suzy, or say, 'Liam will take you home after the race.'

Of course, other people began to think that they were a pair—Suzy was always with Liam, never with Mark—but seeing her with his friend didn't seem to make Mark jealous. On the contrary, it amused him to pull the wool over everyone's eyes. He merely laughed at Suzy's uncertainty and uneasiness.

Suzy soon realised that Liam, too, was uneasy about the game they were playing. She asked him outright one day, 'Do you think Mark's wrong to lie to his mother?' and Liam had brusquely agreed.

'He's a coward. He ought to face her with the truth, not keep ducking it. Her sort of possessive feeling keeps on growing. She's young enough to marry again, but she won't, not while she has Mark.' Liam was very fond of Mrs Culloch, despite her jealous love of her son. He had known her since he was a small boy himself and had often stayed at the Culloch home during his school holidays if his own parents were away. 'This way, both their lives are being ruined.'

'I'm sorry for her,' Suzy began, but Liam shook his head.

'Don't be. If you must be sorry for anyone, be sorry for yourself. Why do you think Mark picked you out at once? He's using you, because you're strong and he hopes you'll take on his mother for him.'

Suzy had stared in disbelief. 'Strong? Me?' That

was one adjective she would never have applied to herself. 'You can't be serious; I'm not strong.'

Liam had laughed shortly. 'Aren't you?' He had encircled her wrist with the fingers of one hand, the bracelet tightning until she gave a gasp of protest. 'Physically, perhaps not, but in every real sense you're stronger than Mark has ever been. His mother couldn't have held on to him for so long if he hadn't been so weak. Mark has a problem, he thinks you'll solve it for him.' He'd lifted a finger to her mouth and traced the line of it. 'You are in love with him, aren't you?'

'Yes,' she said, startled—didn't he realise that she and Mark were going to marry?

'Pity,' Liam had said, then suddenly bent his head and kissed her hard until she put both hands against his powerful chest and pushed him away. Then he was gone, his mouth crooked with derision, shrugging.

After that it had changed between them. Suzy had become shy and wary and Liam had kept his distance, their casual friendliness a thing of the past. And in its place was an awareness she felt even when they were laughing over some joke or talking to other people at a party. Suzy saw far too much of him and far too little of Mark. She didn't plan it that way; over the weeks it made her more and more uneasy. She felt like someone drifting inexorably further and further from safety, yet unable to get back to dry land. When she was with Mark she tried to hint at her anxiety, but

Mark didn't want to listen. He wanted her to comfort, not disturb, him.

Her memories of that time were all of Liam; of a snowy January day when they walked through crystalline woods making the first human tracks on virgin paths and seeing the delicate prints of birds and rabbits and the occasional fox among the white-dusted bracken and the trees which were decked with glittering white, acres of Christmas trees under a cold blue sunlit sky. Liam had flung a snowball at her and she had run, laughing, a cherry-red woollen cap on her blonde hair, a woollen scarf that matched it floating behind her. Liam had grabbed at the scarf and held the two ends, tethering her like a plunging pony, then pulled her towards him. For a second he had almost kissed her, and she had wanted him to so badly, then he had released her and walked on in silence, and Suzy had slept very badly that night.

She hated the parties now: the lowered lights, the sweet music, and herself in Liam's arms, her cheek sometimes brushing his, her arms round his neck while their bodies moved intimately, far too intimately. He tried not to look at her too often; she tried not to watch him. They stopped talking, they rarely laughed. They fought hard not to touch each other, but when they danced their bodies clung of their own volition.

It was at a party that Suzy met Reno, an Italian driver with a shock of black hair and a cheerful grin. His English was terrible, and when he discovered that Suzy spoke a little Italian he latched on to her that

evening, monopolising her, impervious to hints from
Suzy that she wasn't free. Liam didn't show up until
very late; Mark had been with his mother and unable
to intervene, although he had watched Suzy and
Reno sullenly across the room. When Liam got there,
Mark muttered something to him, scowling, and
Liam had come across to where Suzy and Reno were
dancing and separated them by brute force.

He spoke Italian too. Suzy didn't quite grasp
everything he said, but Reno threw up his hands,
gabbling, and Liam hit him.

It was all over in a moment, but Liam took her
home then, as if she was a disgraced schoolgirl, and
Suzy grew angry, turning on him in her flat as he was
about to go back to the party.

'Don't ever make a scene like that again! I'm not
your property!'

'Mark . . .' he began, and she turned a scalding red
with anger.

'If Mark didn't like to see me dancing with another
man, he should have danced with me himself! I'm
tired of this hole-and-corner love affair. If Mark
loved me, he'd have told his mother the truth long
ago.'

'Is that why you flirted with the Italian?' Liam had
asked, his face harsh. 'Trying to make Mark jealous?'

She had stared at him, knowing that she didn't
really care what Mark felt. It had been Liam who
mattered for weeks now.

'How far were you prepared to go?' Liam had
demanded. 'All the way? Reno probably expected you

to go back to his room after the party.'

'At least he was frank about what he wanted,' Suzy had muttered, very flushed. Night after night she had danced close to Liam, held tightly in his arms in smoky, shadowy rooms, and Liam's body had signalled desire as blatantly as the lively Italian had done yet Liam had never said a word or tried to come any closer.

Liam had turned a dark, angry red, staring at her without answering.

'I'm so sick of secret fantasies!' Suzy had snapped. 'You told me yourself that Mark was using me—I don't believe he cares a damn about me and I don't care a ...'

Liam had put a hand over her mouth, his eyes brooding and intense. 'Mark's my oldest friend,' he had said huskily.

She had stared up at him over the muffling fingers, her lips trembling against his flesh, and he had said, 'He trusts me not to take you from him.' Then he had groaned. 'Damn Mark, he had no right to put me in this position! I should never have agreed to play his crazy game.' His hand had dropped and she had waited with a heavy-beating heart, knowing he was going to kiss her.

'Suzy,' he had whispered hoarsely. 'Oh, God, Suzy, I didn't want to feel this way about you, but it's too late to stop now.'

Her heart had turned over, feeling him stare at her mouth with a hunger that matched her own.

'Mark should have told his mother long ago,' she

had said. 'He kept me hidden for too long. I stopped loving him, all the feeling vanished, and I can only feel sorry for him now.'

'Are you sure? You have to be quite sure, Suzy,' Liam had said and when she nodded he had pulled her into his arms. The emotion she had been suppressing since the first time he kissed her leapt up like a forest fire. She wanted him with a sensuality and need she had never felt for Mark, because with Mark there had always been too much held back on both sides; he was too afraid to love her.

'I've wanted you for so long,' Liam had whispered. 'I've gone out of my mind, just looking at you and wanting to do this . . .' His hands had moved and she had moaned, her eyes shut tight, giving herself without hesitation. Liam had carried her into her bedroom and they had made love; he had stayed all night and she had woken up in his arms, their naked bodies merging even then, his pressed closely into her back, his hands clasped around her, his face buried in her shoulder.

She had turned, sighing with pleasure, cuddling closer, and Liam had looked sombrely at her.

'We shouldn't have done this,' he had said. 'How the hell can we tell Mark? He trusted me to keep my hands off you. The race next week is the most important of the year; we can't tell him until after that, it might ruin his chance of winning.'

Suzy had turned pale, facing the tangle of three lives which they would have to unravel before they could openly claim each other.

'You'll tell him after the race, though?' she had whispered and Liam had nodded, but of course after the race he hadn't wanted to break the news to Mark because it had been Liam who won that race and the competitive spirit which was so much part of both men had made it impossible for Liam to tell his oldest friend that not only had he beaten him in that race, he had stolen his girl, too.

Mark had gone abroad with his mother for several weeks. Suzy had understood why Liam felt he had to wait for the right moment, but she was sick of secrets, furtive meetings, pretence. She was on edge until Mark was back in England, but it soon became clear that Liam still hesitated about telling him, and Mark, of course, expected to pick up his relationship with Suzy where he had left off. He rang to make a date with her two days after his return, his voice far too cheerful for him to have heard the truth from Liam.

She saw him for the last time, trying to break the news gently, and Mark had reacted with the tell-tale signs of violent rage she had learnt to fear. 'I'll kill him!' he broke out. 'The bastard! The minute my back was turned he took you ...'

'No, Mark,' she'd said, very pale. In that mood, Mark was terrifying.

'Have you slept with him?' he'd asked, and her face had betrayed her. Mark had hit her so hard he knocked her across the room, then he had gone in search of Liam, his face twisted with fury. Liam had been at his Sevenoaks cottage that day. He had begun to drive to London and Mark had passed him on a quiet Kentish road, doing an abrupt U-turn with a screech of tyres in order to pursue him, the blaring of his horn forcing Liam to pull into a lay-by.

Suzy had no idea what they had said to each other, Liam had lied at the inquest, saying only that Mark had been angry over some remark he had made and had challenged him to prove himself a better driver. Liam had driven away and Mark had gone after him; it had become a race along the motorway at speeds which were dangerously reckless until Mark's car hit a patch of oil on the tarmac. Spinning out of control, it went through a wall and burst into flames. Mark was killed on impact, the police surgeon told the inquest, but for Suzy that had been little comfort. She had been in the courtroom and heard the description of the flames, the burnt-out car, and in her nightmares Mark was never dead; surrounded by flames, he called her, accused her.

She had last seen Liam that day in the court, his face white and frozen. She had known it was all over between herself and Liam. Liam's eyes had told her that he blamed her; *she* had told Mark, *she* had caused his death. They hadn't spoken, nor had she seen him again until the day he came to Alex's cottage.

When Liam wrote his book he had disguised the truth by altering most of the circumstances and characters just enough to make them unrecognisable. He had left Mark's mother out of the story altogether and the fatal crash had happened on a racetrack, not on a motorway, but the emotional triangle was there, the two race-drivers and the girl they both wanted, the girl whose character Suzy knew was based on herself, but so bitterly twisted by Liam's interpretation that she had been shocked when she read it.

She stared down the misty, rainy Embankment at the gleam of the gun-metal river and beyond that the lit windows of office blocks on the other bank of the Thames, her eyes seeing nothing of any of the view, her heart aching.

'Do you want coffee or don't you?' asked Carina irritably, and Suzy started, looking round.

'Sorry?'

'I've asked you three times—do you want coffee?' They were both staring at her and Suzy flushed under their scrutiny.

'Oh, yes, thank you. Black, please.' She met Liam's eyes bleakly, wondering why he had insisted on her presence here at this meeting. She hadn't contributed anything; she had hardly even heard a word they said, although their discussion of the book had run through her own thoughts like a dark undercurrent, prompting memories, reminding her of unassuaged desire.

'So, we start work properly on Friday morning,' said Carina. 'My flat, ten o'clock sharp.' Her voice was light, warm, flirtatious, and Liam's voice sounded the same note when he answered.

'I'll look forward to that.'

'I can see you're going to be a good pupil,' Carina teased.

'Oh, I intend to be the best you've ever had,' he murmured mockingly, and Carina laughed, a crackle of electricity between them.

Suzy drank her black coffee and said nothing, jealousy eating her as she recognised the double meanings in what they were saying to each other. Was that why Liam had insisted on her being present? Had he wanted her to know that he intended to have an affair with Carina? His hostility to herself was almost tangible; every time their eyes met she felt Liam hating her, and a burning sense of injustice rose up in her throat,

He was blaming her for everything—not merely for Mark's death but for their brief affair before that. The portrait of her in his book had made that crystal-clear, and Carina had underlined it just now. Suzy felt sick every time she thought about what Carina had said. It wasn't true; she wasn't a bitch or a cold-hearted tease who used men. Liam had no right to paint her like that.

'God, look at the time—must dash, I'm having tea with a Royal Academician who wants me to ghost his memoirs. Terribly dreary, poor darling, but he's paying me a hefty old fee. See you on Friday, Liam.'

Suzy half rose, startled, but Carina was already hurrying away and Liam's hand shot out and gripped Suzy's wrist, urging her back into her seat.

'I haven't paid the bill. My car's parked on the side road leading to the Embankment—I'll give you a lift back to the office.'

'I'm not going back to the office,' Suzy said in agitation. She didn't want to be alone with him. 'I'm going home. I . . .' She thought wildly and could only come up with a weak excuse. 'I've got a headache.'

He eyed her derisively. 'Oh, dear, how sad!'

Her flush deepened and she was about to snap back at him when the waiter approached with the bill. Suzy sank back, brooding, fully intending to walk out of the hotel and get a taxi as soon as Liam's attention was elsewhere, but he wrote a cheque with one eye on her and then coolly guided her out of the hotel without giving her a chance to escape. It had stopped raining, the sky was a fresh, tender blue and the sun was shining as they walked down towards the Embankment.

'I can get a taxi,' Suzy said irritably, attempting to pull free.

'Do you usually skip off halfway through the day?' Liam countered. 'Does Alex Stevenson know you only do a morning's work?'

Suzy stopped and lifted her arm, showing him her watch. 'It's nearly four o'clock, for your information. By the time I got back to Wardour Street it would be half past four and I leave at five, anyway, while Alex is away, because there simply isn't anything for me to do. When he is here, I often don't get away until six-thirty or seven and some evenings I may work even later, if Alex needs a secretary after he's been filming all day. He doesn't expect me to clockwatch then—why should he mind me leaving early when my work's finished?'

Liam regarded her coolly. 'That was a very impassioned speech about nothing in particular. I wonder why you're in such an angry mood?'

'You know why!' she said, trembling with violent emotion. 'You've crucified me in your book—I'm nothing like that girl, nothing at all!'

'No?' he asked, one brow rising sardonically. 'Then how come you know it's meant to be you?'

'I . . . because . . .' she stammered, and he laughed, turning to unlock his car.

'Nobody likes their own reflection in a mirror,' he said drily, turning back, and Suzy began to walk away fast, too angry to answer that.

Liam grabbed her, forcibly bundled her into the front seat of the car and slammed the door on her. He was next to her before she had pulled herself together and while she was trying to open the door he leaned over and deftly clipped the seatbelt across her.

'Just sit there and be quiet,' he said, starting the engine. 'You can tell me what you think of me later, when we've got more time.'

He pulled away from the kerb and she froze, watching his profile warily, her ears buzzing with hypertension. What had he meant by that?

CHAPTER FIVE

SINKING back into her seat, Suzy stared ahead, her mind awash with angry thoughts. She had been puzzled by his insistence that she make a third at that lunch with Carina; at times during the meal she had wondered if he was tormenting her by making it clear that he was embarking on an affair with the other woman, but now she was sure that the real reason for her own presence had been so that Liam could watch her squirm as he and Carina discussed the girl in his book.

It hadn't been enough for Liam to etch her portrait with vitriol; he had needed to watch her face as she reacted to what he'd done.

Three years ago, she had believed herself in love with him; but she hadn't really known him at all, had she? She had fallen for his image; the loose-limbed, daring driver whose panache was a byword on the track. She hadn't suspected for an instant that he had a cruel streak, a taste for sadism. She wouldn't have believed it if anyone had told her that Liam enjoyed inflicting pain, but during lunch he had watched her, smiling, eyes mocking, and she wished she had been able to hide the hurt she felt. She hadn't; she hadn't hidden anything.

Her mind was beginning to run ahead and guess the bleak future. If this film was made, that portrait of her would have an enormous audience. What if someone did know about her and Mark? She would be branded and there would be no way she could prove herself innocent of the charges Liam had brought. He had put her in the dock and sentenced her, and she was helpless to defend herself—he had pointed that out to her just now. Merely to admit that she recognised the character was some sort of plea of guilty as charged.

Oh, Liam was clever, she thought grimly. He had trapped her. She couldn't see a way out; pain was building up inside her as he pulled up at the kerb outside her home. She fumbled with the safety-belt and hurriedly opened the door, hoping to get away before he caught up with her, but of course he was on the pavement, waiting for her, as she made for the front entrance of the building.

'I thought you were going to tell me what you think of me?' he mocked.

'It would take too long!' Suzy ground out, pushing his hands away as he reached for her.

'I've got all night,' he said, his tone silky with threat, and then he ran a speculative glance down over her and Suzy's face began to burn.

'I'd rather die!' she snapped, suddenly realising that one of her neighbours was walking towards them and watching them with curiosity.

'You're home early, Suzy,' the other girl said, but she was staring at Liam, eyes wide and fascinated. Suzy could almost see him in those dilated pupils: tall and powerful with ruffled black hair and rugged features, a very masculine man with a tiny white scar above one cheekbone where he had once been accidentally slashed in a fencing match. No wonder Janet was staring.

'It's a lovely evening after all that rain this morning,' the girl said to Liam, who answered as calmly as if he and Suzy had been having some academic discussion.

'Let's hope this weather stays around for a few days.'

'Oh, that would be nice,' Janet agreed fulsomely. 'You haven't moved into the flats, have you?' She sounded wistful, expecting a negative reply, and sighed faintly when she got one.

'No, I'm just visiting Suzy'. Liam slid a hand through Suzy's arm and she tensed at the touch. 'Well, we'd better go and start getting the supper,' he said lightly. 'Nice to have met you.'

'Nice to have met *you*,' said Janet, her curly brown hair framing a flushed, regretful oval face, as Suzy shot her a glance and a wry wave.

As Suzy hunted for her front door key she muttered to Liam, 'What supper? I didn't invite you for supper. We've only just had lunch.'

'Give that to me,' he said, taking the key from her shaky fingers as she fumbled with it. He unlocked the door and propelled her into the flat, then coolly walked into the sitting-room and flung himself down on the couch, stretching out full length with his hands crossed behind his head.

'Make yourself at home,' Suzy said bitterly, watching him from the safety of the door.

'Have you got anything to drink? A cognac or . . .'

'No, I haven't. This isn't a hotel. I don't know what

you think you're doing, walking in here, pushing me around . . .'

'I'm making myself comfortable . . .' he drawled.

'I can see that. I want to know why . . .'

'Before you start telling me what you think of me,' he ended as if she hadn't spoken. 'It would help to have a stiff drink too!'

Suzy glared at him, taking off her raincoat and flinging it across a chair. 'Why don't you just go away and leave me alone? That's all I want.'

'Is it?' he asked in that silky, mocking voice, his grey eyes moving over her in a way that made her feel weak and threatened. 'All you want, Suzy? Sure about that?'

'Get out,' she whispered, the hair standing up on the back of her neck.

He laughed softly. 'You get very nervous whenever we're alone. I wonder why.'

'I'm not nervous, I'm angry,' she said, wishing it was true. Liam was too shrewd, too quick to read her feelings; it frightened and unnerved her.

'Angry?' he repeated, and came off the couch so rapidly that Suzy went into a panic and backed across the little corridor into the kitchen. Liam strode towards her and kept coming until she had backed herself into a corner by the fridge.

He loomed over her, his face grim. 'You're angry? What right do you think you have to be angry?'

'Your book . . .' she stammered, her throat raw as he came so close.

'My book was honest, which is more than I can say for you!'

She flinched, 'You have no right to say that!'

'I have every right.' He grabbed her arms and shook her like a rag doll; her ash-blonde hair flung to and fro across her pale face, half-blinding her. 'You used me!' he ground out between his clenched teeth. 'I was your cat's-paw, wasn't I? You couldn't get Mark to propose and make the engagement public, so you deliberately started an affair with me to make him jealous enough to be ready to risk a showdown with his mother!'

The floor seemed to come up and hit her. Dazed and appalled she stood there, swaying, for a few seconds, staring at him without being able to speak. At last she managed to whisper rustily, 'No! It isn't true. No.'

'Don't lie to me, you little bitch!' grated Liam, looking at her as if he hated her.

'I'm not lying! You've twisted the facts and made them mean something else. Mark *was* afraid of telling his mother about me, but you know I'd fallen out of love with Mark long before the crash!'

'Do I?' His mouth took on a bitter curve—not quite a smile; far too angry. 'So you told me at the time, but then you wanted to have me dancing on a string so that you could jolt Mark into telling his mother. And I wonder if you were ever really in love with either of us. Mark's family had all that lovely money, was that what you were really after?'

Her eyes widened in surprise; she felt a terrible drumming in her ears, as if she was going to faint.

'Money?' she whispered. 'I don't know what you're talking about.'

'No, of course not,' he mocked coldly. 'You didn't know Mark's mother was a rich woman and that he was living on an allowance from her, or that if she turned against him and cut him off he'd have to give up racing?'

She weakly shook her head, feeling it was too heavy for her neck just as she felt that her legs were too weak to support her for much longer. She was almost hanging from Liam's angry hands; he was holding her up, whether he knew it or not.

'Yes,' Liam insisted when she didn't get a word out. 'You knew and you were determined to kill two birds with one stone, weren't you? By making Mark jealous, you were going to get him to give up racing and announce your engagement—his mother might not have been very happy about Mark marrying, but she would have been over the moon about him giving up racing, and that shrewd little brain of yours had worked out that she would be ready to forgive him for the marriage out of sheer gratitude to you for persuading him not to race.'

Dumbly, Suzy shook her head. It wasn't true, any of it. Why was he making this up?

'That's what you were up to, wasn't it?'

'No, no, no!' she managed unsteadily. 'Why are you saying all this? What on earth makes you think I'd be so scheming and two-faced?'

Dark red rushed up his face and he shook her again, bending towards her, his features convulsed with rage. 'Mark told me! That day, he told me when he forced me off the road. He said he was going to give up racing and tell his mother about you and you'd be married, that was what you wanted, and you'd used me to make him jealous. That was all it had been, a game with me as your pawn ...'

'And you believed him?' she asked, ice-cold with incredulity.

Liam's lips curled back in a snarl, showing her his teeth clenched, the bitter rigidity of his features sending shock waves through her.

After a long silence he said, 'Not at first. We had a blazing row. He followed me down the road, his horn going, ramming me. I had to put on speed, trying to get away from him. He was out of his mind; I think he wanted to force me into crashing. I didn't intend that race, it just happened, and he was killed and I ran into a telegraph pole, and ended up in hospital, facing a prison sentence.' He paused, breathing hard, staring at her. 'And where were you, you lying little bitch? You didn't come to see me in hospital, you didn't write or ring, you just vanished into thin air, and after a few days, I knew Mark had told me the truth. I was just a weapon to use against Mark, and once he was dead you had no further use for me.'

'That isn't true! I didn't come to see you after the crash because I was too stunned with shock. I felt guilty, can't you see that? And when I did come to the hospital they told me I couldn't see you, only relatives could be admitted.'

He stared at her in frozen disbelief, and she saw that he didn't believe her. Tears sprang into her eyes.

'The last time I saw Mark I told him I loved you and it was all over between him and me. I didn't ask him to give up racing and tell his mother about me, he lied to you. I made it crystal clear that everything was over between us.'

'And Mark reacted just the way you knew he would,' Liam drawled, his brows arched and dismissive. 'He was as possessive as his mother, in his own way, and as competitive as hell into the bargain—you knew that. You knew he wouldn't let you go. That was what was so clever, the wide-eyed pretence that he had lost you. Your tactics were very subtle. I congratulate you. I'd no idea you were such a clever psychologist!'

'No! Listen to me . . .' she began, and he shook his head, his eyes insulting.

'I listened to you once and you made a fool of me. I won't listen to you again. Whatever you may say now, the fact is that after the crash you didn't want to know about me and that proved everything that Mark had said about you.'

Suzy put her hand up to his face, holding it while she looked pleadingly into those angry eyes. 'Liam, how can you believe that I didn't mean it when I said I loved you? Have you forgotten the night you took me home after that party? Do you really think I'm the type of girl who sleeps around? You were the first man I'd ever slept with, you know that.'

'Men have been fooled about that before,' he said cynically. 'If you're clever enough to make me believe you loved me, you're clever enough to make me believe that you were a virgin until then.'

Her body throbbed with pain and she closed her eyes, her teeth biting into her inner lip. His cruelty was unbearable; for a moment she couldn't get a word out, then she whispered, 'Go away, please, just go away.'

He didn't move and the silence held a tension which ate at her nerves until she opened her eyes to look at him; she had to know what he was thinking. He was still standing very close, watching her, Suzy's stomach churned with sexual awareness at the look on his taut face.

'Even knowing the truth about you,' he said thickly, 'I still want you. I'll never feel any love for you again, you lying little cheat, but I can't seem to stop wanting you.' He wasn't touching her now; his hands were hanging at his sides, screwed into fists as if to stop himself from lifting them towards her. She saw darkness in his eyes, a leaping black flame that scorched down over her from head to foot. 'Now,' he muttered. 'I want you now!'

Suzy felt a bitter taste in her throat, a sickness and recoil from the contemptuous desire in those eyes. She stared at him fixedly, shaking her head, her lips parting to say, 'No!' No sound emerged, but Liam laughed shortly.

'Still lying, still cheating,' he mocked icily. 'You pretend to say no, but your body says something very different.' He lifted one hand and she drew a painful breath as his fingers lightly stroked her throat and followed the line of her shoulder until it slid down her breast and cupped it softly, warmly. Suzy trembled, watching his face with uncertainty and pain; he hated her and despised her, yet his hands were so gentle, their slow movements intensely seductive.

'Don't,' she pleaded, but she didn't push him away

and in the coaxing hand she felt her nipples hardening and her flesh burning, and knew Liam could feel it too.

He lowered his head very slowly and she stood on tiptoe to meet his mouth, her arms going round his neck. Whatever else happened, she needed that kiss, just one, a salve for the pain he had given her, some comfort after the way he had torn her apart. She kissed him hungrily, her fingers twisting in his thick warm hair, her body surrendered and shaking in his arms.

Liam suddenly pushed her away and stood back, his face harsh. 'Yes, I could have you, don't try to deny it. But it wouldn't mean a thing, because sexual satisfaction when you despise yourself for taking it just leaves a nasty taste in the mouth!'

Suzy hit him without stopping to think, her hand stinging as it dropped from his face.

A dark red mark glowed on his cheek; she heard the rasp of his breathing and tensed, expecting him to hit her back, but those hard grey eyes merely flashed down over her and dismissed her, then Liam turned on his heel and walked out.

Suzy heard him go into the sitting-room and collect his coat, then the front door slammed. He was gone, but the air was resonant with all the bitter things he had said to her. She walked shakily down the corridor to the bathroom and turned on the shower; she felt unclean, she wanted to wash away all the shame and anger and fear Liam had made her feel. Stripping with unsteady fingers, she stood under the jet of water, her eyes closed, unable to rid herself of the memory of the last half-hour. Liam had meant to hurt her, and he had succeeded.

She wasn't hungry and she couldn't relax enough to read or watch television, so she curled up on the couch and went to sleep, but her nightmare woke her just as the sun went down, and she sat up, shuddering, to find the sitting-room bathed in rosy light, as if the sky was on fire, as if her dream of the burning car had taken over her physical world. It was too much; Suzy burst into tears and cried until she had no more tears to shed.

Next day she felt totally empty, but calm; nothing seemed to matter any more, she worked automatically, refusing to think—that made life so much easier; you just put one foot in front of another and kept on going, like a robot. Staring into the mirror in the cloakroom after lunch, she was surprised to see flesh and blood reflected back and turned away hurriedly before her cauterised nerve-ends could begin to feel again.

To keep herself busy she decided to reorganise part of the filing system, and was knee-deep in dusty old files when the office door opened and a thin, chic, bright-eyed figure appeared.

'Hello, Suzy, how are you?'

'Oh, Mrs Jonas ... I'm fine, thank you, how are you?' Suzy was completely thrown off balance by finding herself face to face with the legendary Leah Jonas in one of the incredibly smart outfits she had designed for herself. Suzy thought that it would be difficult to say what made the trouser suit so stunning; the cut was simple, the lines were fluid and economic, the colour a warm pinky gold. Suzy couldn't account for the way it looked, but maybe it was the way Leah wore it. She had once described herself as the only stick insect in the designer business, but that didn't begin to capture her extraordinary looks. Her hair was blue; it had been black when she was young, but when she began to go grey she had it dyed first pink, then green, and now a delicate shade of blue. Her face was hauntingly bony : deep eye-sockets and a high bridged nose, angular cheekbones and a sharp jawline. Her eyes were black and huge; she wore heavy eye make-up, Egyptian, drawing you away from the lines of laughter around her mouth. If you saw her briefly at a distance you would never guess in a million years that Leah Jonas was eighty.

Gazing at the litter of files, Leah asked plaintively, 'Anywhere for me to sit down?' and Suzy rushed to clear a chair, dusting it apologetically.

'Mrs Jonas, you know Alex isn't here . . .'

'Of course I do. My husband has driven down to see him today.' Leah waved a tiny, claw-like hand. 'Can you stop all that and come and sit and talk, Suzy? I would like some black coffee too, if you can find some.'

Distracted, Suzy nodded, moving to the door. 'Of course, I won't be a moment—sugar?'

'I don't take it, my dear.' The great panda eyes gazed back at her as if Leah Jonas could read her mind, and Suzy backed out. Why was Mrs Jonas here? They had met quite often a year ago when Leah designed the clothes for a film Alex was making, a futuristic film set on a distant planet. Leah had produced the most incredible clothes; they would create a sensation when the film came out. She was a famous designer; her label could be found all over the civilised world and her business had a yearly turnover in millions. Although she had no children, her marriage to the boss of Empire Films had been a very happy one. They were both legends, Leah and Leonard Jonas. They circled each other like two great golden suns, each with a host of satellites glittering after them; their orbits interlocked yet never clashed. Suzy knew that each was proud of what the other had achieved.

What on earth could Leah Jonas want to talk to her about? Suzy made the coffee rapidly and went back with it. Handing a mug to Mrs Jonas, she sat down opposite and asked politely, 'How can I help you, Mrs Jonas?'

'Tell me about Liam Moor,' the older woman said, taking her breath away.

Swallowing, Suzy lowered her head to hide the flush rising in her face and sipped her coffee, giving herself time to think. Did Mrs Jonas know anything?

Huskily, she asked, 'What do you want to know about him? He's written a book which Alex wants to buy, he was a racing driver. There isn't much to know about him other than that.'

Leah Jonas gave her a wry little grin. 'My dear, one of my particular gifts is a photographic memory. When I first met you, I knew at once that I'd seen you before, but I couldn't think where for some time, then I remembered. I'd seen you having dinner with someone in a restaurant some years earlier. Oh, I might not have noticed or remembered you if I hadn't been with a racing car buff. He stared at the man you were with and told us, "That's Liam Moor!". The way he said it made me laugh; it was as if he was saying, there's St George. Complete reverence; it made me stare at you both—it made me curious.'

Suzy bit her lip. 'Oh ... I see. I'm afraid I didn't notice you.'

Leah smiled. 'I'm sure you didn't. You weren't noticing anything but the man you were with.' She drank some coffee and then said gently, 'I never mentioned it to you because it didn't seem important. I don't believe in prying into people's private lives unless it's necessary.'

Suzy met her eyes directly. 'And you think it's necessary now?'

The old woman nodded, her face coaxing. 'My dear, Alex has told my husband that it was you who brought this book to his notice. My husband is very anxious because Alex seems to be behaving in an uncharacteristic fashion, talking to the author before he's even raised the matter with the company, commissioning Mr Moor to write the script and trying to stampede us into paying far more for these rights than they're really worth. My husband is afraid Alex isn't himself, that his illness has temporarily unsettled his grasp on reality ...'

'Oh, that's ridiculous!' Suzy burst out, very flushed. 'I talked to Alex last weekend and he's perfectly normal. There's nothing wrong with his grasp on reality.'

'No doubt you're ambitious for your young man
...' began Mrs Jonas, but Suzy interrupted.

'He's not my young man!'

'You forget, I've seen you with him—I may be old,
but I still recognise a woman in love when I see one.'
Mrs Jonas eyed her reprovingly. 'I wouldn't have
guessed that you would play this sort of game, Suzy;
taking advantage of the fact that Alex isn't his usual
self, talking him into buying the rights of your man's
book—that wasn't strictly honest, was it? No, I know
there's nothing illegal about using your influence in
that way, but I'm surprised at you, because I talked to
Alex on the phone myself and I know you haven't
declared your interest. Alex doesn't know about you
and Mr Moor, now, does he?'

Suzy put down her coffee mug, all the colour
flowing out of her face. 'No, he doesn't, and there *isn't*
anything any more—I haven't seen Liam for three
years, Mrs Jonas. It's over, and I assure you that far
from my bringing the book to Alex's attention, it was
purely accidental that he picked up my copy. He
thought it was a present for him, but I'd bought it for
myself. I wasn't trying to interest Alex in Liam. I
wish to God Alex had never seen the book, and in fact
I've been trying to nerve myself up to giving notice so
that I needn't see Liam any more. You've got it all
wrong.'

Mrs Jonas studied her closely, frowning. 'I don't
know whether to believe you or not,' she said slowly.
'I admit, I was shaken when I thought you'd behaved
so deceitfully with Alex. I've always prided myself on
reading people's characters and it was a shock to think

I was wrong about you.' She leaned forward, her eyes holding Suzy's. 'Why is your relationship with Mr Moor over?' She watched the tide of colour rising in the girl's face again and sighed. 'Forgive me, my dear, I see it's a painful question—but I must know the answer, I'm afraid, if I'm to believe you.'

Staring at the desk, Suzy stammered through a brief explanation and Mrs Jonas listened intently.

'Men are such fools,' she said wryly, when Suzy fell silent. 'Very well, my dear. I do believe you, but I think you should have told Alex that you knew Mr Moor. Sooner or later, he's going to find out, and when he does he's going to suspect what I suspected—that you used him. Alex will not be very happy about that. I think you'd better tell him as soon as possible and then, perhaps, you should ask for a transfer to another office.'

Suzy looked bleakly at her, nodding. 'Very well,' she agreed. At least it would take her out of Liam's orbit; she wouldn't have to see him again.

CHAPTER SIX

SUZY didn't feel she could tell Alex the truth over the phone, nor could she put it in a letter—it was all too personal and too involved. She had to tell him face to face, which meant that it would have to wait until Alex came up to London a week later. He and Sara were stopping in town for a couple of nights on their way down to Southampton to board a cruise ship bound for the Bahamas.

'I want to get him away before L.J. talks him into going back to work,' Sara Stevenson had told Suzy, and she had apparently succeeded. They would be away for three weeks, sailing out there and flying home. Knowing Alex, Suzy couldn't help applauding Sara and at the same time wondering how on earth Alex's wife was going to make sure he stayed in the Bahamas when he arrived there. He had already been off work for weeks; the fitter he got, the more he was likely to fidget restlessly and think about his work.

She said as much to Clarrie that weekend and her sister laughed. 'Look, any woman who can make a success out of marriage to a live-wire like Alex Stevenson is very smart. I've no doubt she still has a trick or two up her sleeve. Didn't you say she was attractive?'

'I'm sure I said she was beautiful,' Suzy said drily. 'Not to mention very sexy. How else do you think she caught Alex's eye?'

'A second honeymoon in the Bahamas, tropical moon, soft music and warm nights—you don't really think he'll get tired of all that, do you?' Clarrie said wickedly, and Suzy smiled agreement. No doubt Sara *would* think of ways of keeping Alex's mind off work.

She was babysitting for her sister again that Saturday night, but Clarrie seemed almost discontented when Suzy assured her she didn't mind staying in with the children that evening.

'You should be out with a man, not babysitting for me!'

'Don't you want me to babysit?' Suzy teased, and was given an impatient look.

'You know what I mean! It isn't natural to go on grieving; living like a widow ...'

'I'm not!' Suzy protested flushing.

'Then where are the men in your life? Produce one! There must be some men working at Empire Films who aren't married.'

'Yes, and I had lunch with one of them the other day,' Suzy said, shamelessly using poor Joshua.

'Who? Tell!' Clarrie was on the scent at once; her nose quivering, her eyes interested.

'Oh, go to this film. My private life isn't your business,' Suzy said crossly and Derek chimed in firmly from the doorway.

'My view exactly. Clarissa, if you don't come now we'll miss the last show and I'll be in a bad temper all weekend. I've been looking forward to this Clint Eastwood film for ages.'

Reluctantly, Clarrie departed, but she gave her

sister a threatening look as she went. She hadn't given up on the subject yet; the enquiry was merely postponed.

Suzy was staying the night, so after watching television for a short time she made herself some cocoa and went to bed. The children were all fast asleep, the house was quiet and her thoughts clamorous. She was very glad she had never told Clarrie about Liam; she would have had no peace once Liam reappeared in her life. Her sister would have pestered her with questions about him, Clarrie was quite tireless in her absorption in other people's lives; she felt that having made such a success of her own she was well qualified to give advice to everyone else.

On the Sunday morning, Suzy was up early with the three children so that their parents could sleep late after getting back in the early hours of the morning. Clarrie and Derek had been to a late film show and then gone on to a Chinese meal. Suzy wasn't surprised when they didn't surface until lunchtime on that Sunday. She had cooked lunch, with the children's assistance; it would have been far easier without their help, but it kept them all happy in the kitchen, out of earshot of their sleeping parents. The two older children stood on chairs at the sink washing the small new potatoes and splashing muddy water everywhere. The baby sat in her highchair gnawing a peeled carrot and banging a spoon.

It was, thought Suzy, a happy domestic scene, but that was until William trickled water on his younger brother's head and Derry screamed blue murder, making Anna start to cry, throwing her spoon away and kicking her plump pink legs wildly. It took Suzy ten minutes to restore calm and by then Clarrie had come downstairs, yawning and pink-faced from sleep.

'Oh, you angel—lunch smells gorgeous! Hello, boys. William, don't pull Derry's hair, that isn't kind.' Clarrie picked up the baby and kissed her damp face. 'Have you been crying for Mummy? Poor little lamb! She's bubbling again; those horrid teeth hurting, are they? Never mind.' Clarrie smoothed the baby's soft hair and prowled over to the oven, sniffing. 'When will the chicken be ready? I'd better tell Derek to hurry up; he's just going to have a bath.'

'No hurry, I timed it for one o'clock. Did you sleep well?'

'Like a log,' said Clarrie, yawning again.

Suzy envied her; she had slept badly, fitfully, waking several times from a bad dream, although it had only once been the recurring nightmare about the car crash in which Mark died. The other times she had been dreaming of Liam, finding herself in his arms and aching with passion even though she knew that he was making love to her with contempt as well as desire.

She didn't tell her sister that she meant to resign from her job with Alex Stevenson; the very thought of Clarrie's probing questions made her shudder. It wasn't going to be easy to tell Alex why she had to leave, but she knew that if she didn't tell him Leah Jonas would do so, and that left her no choice.

The following week began very quietly. She got through the routine work each day without interruption and there was no sign of Liam to disturb her, but she was still on edge as she waited for Alex and Sara Stevenson to arrive in London. Each day brought that moment nearer; each day Suzy grew more nervous.

On the Wednesday she got a phone call from the rights department about a query relating to an earlier film, and while she was talking to the head of rights she asked how the negotiations with Liam Moor were coming along.

'Fairly smoothly since Mr Jonas himself took a hand,' she was told, and her eyes opened wider.

'I didn't know he had.'

'Oh, yes, he's had lunch with Moor and his agent and the major parts are all settled. When is Mr Stevenson coming back to work? Do you know yet?'

'Another month, at least.'

'What exactly was wrong with him? He's been off for weeks. I could do with a nice long holiday myself.' The man rang off irritably and Suzy replaced her phone, frowning. So L.J. had intervened and Alex was definitely buying Liam's book—that meant that she couldn't back out of telling him that she had known Liam well at one time. In some ways, she was going to hate leaving, in others, it would be a relief to go before Alex began making the film.

At least she wouldn't have to go through weeks of anguish seeing Liam every day, feeling him watch her with contempt. Of course, Alex was going to wonder why Liam didn't say a word about their past relationship. He was bound to be curious, even suspicious.

Suzy frowned, biting her lip. Perhaps she ought to

warn Liam that she was going to have to tell Alex? The negotiations over his book weren't finished yet; the company might still back out if Alex went cold on the idea, and when she told Alex her news it was possible that he might feel she and Liam had deliberately tricked him. Mrs Jonas had suspected it, why shouldn't Alex?

Their silence about the past probably did seem a trifle calculated. When people hide something they usually have a very good reason, and there was a great deal at stake in the sale of these film rights. Liam could well earn a fortune from his book if the film was made, not merely from Empire Films but from a vastly inflated sale of the book itself. This would make his name, and, with so much to win or lose, it wouldn't be surprising if Alex and Mr Jonas felt rather differently about the whole project once they realised that it hadn't been pure chance that had put Liam's book into Alex's hands.

Suzy argued with herself for several hours, reluctant to speak to Liam and yet not wishing to ruin his chances of selling the film rights. Eventually, at around four o'clock that afternoon, she dialled his number and waited to hear his voice, her heart beating like a sledge-hammer.

There was no reply. The phone rang on and on, and at last she gave a sigh and was about to hang up when she heard the ringing tone stop and a confused mumble at the other end.

'Hello?' she said, frowning.

'Wha . . .' the thick voice muttered. It couldn't be Liam, she thought; it sounded drunk, even crazy.

'Could I speak to Liam Moor, please?'

'Go 'way!' the voice snarled, and the phone slammed down. Suzy slowly replaced her own phone, staring down at it. Maybe she had dialled the wrong number. She picked up the phone again and dialled. Once more the ringing continued for a long time before someone lifted the phone and she heard the thick mumbling again.

'I want to speak to Liam Moor,' Suzy said, slowly and clearly.

'Well?'

'Liam?' she asked, incredulous.

'Yes, what?' He sounded irritable, angry.

'It's Suzy . . .' she began, and he yelled into the phone.

'Why don't you for heaven's sake leave me alone and let me sleep? Stop haunting me!'

The phone slammed down and she stood there, too shaken to move for several minutes. What was the matter with him? He had sounded drunk. He couldn't be, surely? She looked at her watch; it was a few minutes after four in the afternoon. Had Liam been to lunch with someone and drunk too much wine? He wasn't given to drinking heavily. She put down her own phone and stood staring at nothing, biting her lip.

Was Liam ill? He sounded so strange. If he was drunk, something must have upset him, made him drink too much. Had Mrs Jonas told her husband after all? Had Liam lost his chance of selling the film rights?

She hesitated about doing anything further—he

had made it crystal clear that he didn't want to see her. What was the point of going to see him? He would probably slam the door in her face.

She was anxious enough to put a hand to the phone, meaning to ring again, then she made up her mind. She had to know what was wrong with him. If he wasn't drunk he had to be ill and he might need help, but she wouldn't be able to find out by ringing him. He wasn't making any sense, and she knew she wouldn't be able to rest until she had found out.

She took a taxi to his flat in Camden Town and stood on the pavement outside the Chinese restaurant, staring up at the upper floor on which Liam had his home. Although the daylight hadn't faded yet, his curtains were all closed over the windows.

While she hesitated, a young Chinese girl came out of the restaurant and stared at her. 'You look for someone?'

'Mr Moor,' Suzy told her, and the girl came closer.

'You friend Mr Moor? He sick, very sick, but won't let us call doctor. He not eaten food for two days. My mother very anxious.' The girl was in her teens, slight and rather beautiful, with almond-shaped black eyes and a gentle expression.

'Is your mother here?' asked Suzy, and the girl shook her head.

'No, only me here now. You want key, get into flat? Wait, I get.'

She vanished, and Suzy glanced up at the closed curtains again. What on earth could be wrong with Liam? If he hadn't eaten for several days, it had to be more than a cold, and he couldn't be drunk. A shiver ran down her spine. What could be wrong with him?

The girl came back and unlocked the side door, pointing up the flight of narrow stairs which led to the upper floor.

'Flat up there, OK?'

Suzy nodded. 'Thank you. Are you coming up?'

'So sorry, have to stay in restaurant. If you need some help, please call me.' The girl handed Suzy the front door key, smiling politely, and Suzy began to climb the steep flight of stairs. The building was Victorian and shabby; there was a smell of damp from the plastered walls and the wooden treads under her feet creaked ominously.

Why had Liam chosen to live here? She pushed open the door at the top of the stairs and found herself in a narrow hallway. Liam had carpeted it and painted the walls a warm apricot. Suzy swallowed nervously.

'Liam?' Her voice seemed to echo in the flat as if the place was empty. Nobody seemed to be there at all. She walked slowly towards another door and pushed it open, saying again, 'Liam?'

The room was empty; she stared curiously at the bookshelves lining the walls, the leather-topped desk spread with papers, the leather armchairs and couch. On the whole the room was quite tidy, which surprised her, or perhaps Liam had a cleaner who came in to look after him on a regular basis?

She walked on to the next door and found a narrow galley-like kitchen, everything closely fitted together, using every inch of space. That wasn't tidy; she ran an eye over the cups and glasses littering the draining board, then went on to the door opposite. It was

closed, and she knew Liam was in the room before she
turned the handle. She could hear his breathing,
heavy and stertorous.

She opened the door and stared across the shadowy
space between herself and the bed.

'Liam?'

He didn't stir, so she hesitantly went to the window
and drew back the curtain a little in order to see him
more clearly. He moaned, flinging an arm over his
face as daylight hit it.

'What in God's name . . .'

Suzy stood by the bed, watching his tousled dark
hair, his half-obscured face. As soon as she stood
between him and the light he lowered his arm and
peered at her.

'How do you feel?' Suzy asked huskily, and he
struggled up on to one elbow, his grey eyes gleaming
with fever and something else that made her heart
pick up speed.

'You again—can't I stop dreaming about you?' he
muttered in that thick, husky voice.

She bent over to put a hand on his forehead; it was
red-hot. His temperature must be frighteningly high.
'Liam, how do you feel?' she repeated, wondering if
he was delirious.

'Get into bed and I'll show you,' he said, laughing
wildly and putting a hand up to the nape of her neck
to pull her down on to the bed.

That was when Suzy realised that he was naked.
The sheet fell back and she found herself lying against
his bare chest, the rough dark hair on it brushing her
cheek. She put both hands on his shoulders and

pushed herself up again, holding him down easily enough because his illness had weakened him.

'I'd better call your doctor,' she said unsteadily, not looking at him because she was afraid of her own reaction to what she had just seen; the power and beauty of his body made her tremble. She hadn't forgotten a thing, she found, as if the three years since she last saw him like this had never happened.

Liam lay staring at her, breathing roughly. 'Suzy?' His voice had altered, become sharper, more aware. 'What the hell are you doing here? I thought I was dreaming.'

'Someone from the restaurant downstairs let me in,' she told him, getting to her feet. 'A girl. She was worried about you.'

He frowned, his eyes narrow and glittering. 'Ann Ling? But how did she get hold of you? I've never mentioned you ...'

'I came here because I'd rung you and you sounded odd on the phone,' she said, flushing.

'Then you really did ring? I remember dreaming that I was talking to you on the phone.' He laughed shortly, beads of sweat along his lip. 'I was out of my skull at the time! Sorry if I gave you a fright.'

'I wasn't sure whether you were ill or drunk,' she admitted wryly.

'Both,' he said, his mouth twisting as he glanced at the bedside table. Following that look, Suzy saw the whisky bottle and empty glass. 'The only medicine for a cold,' Liam told her with defiance as she frowned.

'That was stupid of you!' Suzy said crossly. 'And I'm not so sure you do just have a cold. It looks more like 'flu to me. What's your doctor's phone number?'

'I don't want a doctor, it isn't necessary.'

'You're in no fit state to decide what's necessary,' she told him crisply, picking up the bottle of whisky and the glass. She walked out of the room with them and put them in the kitchen and then hunted through the address book she found on Liam's desk until she found his doctor's name and telephone number. She rang the surgery, and the receptionist listened to her description of Liam's symptoms, then said that the doctor would fit him into his rounds that afternoon.

'Dr Kelly won't get there before six, though,' the woman added warningly.

As Suzy put the phone down she heard shuffling movements and the bang of the bathroom door. She went into the bedroom and found the dishevelled bed empty, so she took the opportunity of stripping off the tumbled sheets. Liam came back and leaned in the doorway, supporting himself as if his legs were too weak to hold him up. Giving him a quick secret glance, she saw with relief that he had put on a towelling robe.

'I'll make your bed again in two minutes,' she said over her shoulder. 'Where are the clean sheets?'

'Airing cupboard.' He sounded very tired. She saw him shivering and gave him a frowning look.

'And your pyjamas?'

'Don't wear the damned things. Look, I want to get back into bed.' He took a step towards the chair near the door and swayed; Suzy hurriedly joined him and put an arm around his waist to guide him to the chair. His weight was heavy; she could feel the heat of his

skin through the towelling material. Pushing him into
the chair, she said, 'Sit there until I've made your
bed.'

'Where's my whisky?' he demanded sullenly,
subsiding.

'You've had enough whisky. I'll make you some
hot milk with aspirin in a minute.'

'Bully,' he mumbled. 'Women are born bullies.
Give them an inch and they take a yard.'

As she moved away he put an arm round her waist
and dragged her back, burying his face against her
waist like a child. 'I'm ill, can't you see I'm ill? I'm so
hot.' He was shivering violently; she felt the tremors
running through him as he clutched at her, and
stroked back the tumbled dark hair gently.

'When I've made your bed I'll get you some hot
milk,' she soothed, detaching herself, and he leaned
back in the chair, scowling, watching her make his
bed with a fixed attention that made her uneasy. He
might be ill, but she didn't trust him an inch.

When the bed was made, she turned and said, 'If
the doctor's coming I'd better fetch you some
pyjamas, hadn't I? Where are they?'

'The chest of drawers,' he said, gripping the arms
of his chair and trying to stand. Suzy saw him sway
and hurried over to help. As he finally sank on to the
bed she tried to unlock his arms from her waist, but
Liam laughed softly, his hands linked behind her.

'Does it give you a sense of power? Bossing me
about? Makes you feel superior, does it?'

'Let go and get into bed!' she said sharply,
struggling.

His robe parted and she averted her eyes with a little intake of breath, but a second too late. Liam felt the shock wave sweep over her and leaned forward to bury his face in her throat, kissing her and laughing at the same time.

'You've turned an interesting colour. Why so shocked? You've seen me naked before. You didn't look away then.'

'You're ill and I don't want to catch whatever bug you've picked up!' she said huskily, pushing him away.

He went, shrugging. 'I'm too weak to do anything about it, anyway,' he complained, lying back against the pillows. 'My head's aching and I'm hot one minute and cold the next.'

'So I've noticed,' muttered Suzy, going over to the chest of drawers.

He gave a short laugh. 'Aren't we quick today?'

She threw the pyjamas at him and went out, banging the door behind her. In the kitchen she leaned against the sink, her head hanging, her eyes closed. When he was holding her in his arms she felt complete, real, fully herself in a way she never did when she was with any other man. Even now when she was alone she could experience that powerful emotion merely by remembering the way his mouth had moved against her throat, the husky note in his voice, the sensual movement of his hands on her back. It was insanity to go on loving him when he hated her and only wanted to hurt her; just now he had been needling her again, tormenting her with his smile, his kiss, his touch, knowing what he was doing and mocking her, enjoying her helplessness to resist. Why else was she here now? She had had to come to his flat to find out what was wrong with Liam because she couldn't have slept if she hadn't reassured herself. Instinct had told her he was ill, not drunk; instinct had driven her to come in case he needed her, and Liam's cynical eyes told her that he knew all that and was coldly amused by her emotion.

If she was wise, she would hate him back, but she was a fool and she loved him; she wanted to look after him, to believe he needed her.

She felt wetness on her cheeks and straightened, angrily brushing a hand across her lashes. She would not cry over him. He would see the traces of those tears and smile even more; she would not give him that satisfaction.

A few minutes later she took him the mug of hot milk into which she had crushed some aspirin. Liam watched her through his lashes, the curve of his mouth petulant.

'Do I have to drink this stuff? I hate milk, especially hot milk.'

'I've put some aspirin in it to help lower your temperature.'

'You could have put it in whisky!'

'Milk is better for you.'

'Milk is only good for babies. I'm not a baby!'

'Then stop behaving like one!' she snapped, infuriated, and watched him sulkily drink the milk, then took the mug and turned away. 'Now go back to sleep. I'll wait until the doctor comes.'

'One thing,' he said, settling down again with a

little yawn. 'Can you ring Carina for me? Tell her I can't make our date after all but I'll be in touch later this week.'

Suzy stiffened, jealousy eating away inside her. 'Very well!' she said in a voice she made as blank as possible, then very quietly she closed the bedroom door. Outside she stood there, her body rigid, her teeth tight, her lips drawn back in a soundless scream of rage. When she felt able to, she walked into the sitting-room and looked through Liam's address book again, found Carina's number and dialled it.

The lazy purring voice answered almost at once. 'Hello? Carina Davis speaking.'

'Hello, I've been asked to give you a message from Mr Moor,' Suzy said in a voice devoid of all expression. 'He won't be able to keep his appointment with you, but he'll be in touch as soon as possible.'

'What?' Carina's voice rose shrilly. 'But I've spent the best part of the afternoon cooking duck and cherries and a raspberry surprise! He can't cancel dinner now!'

'Sorry, I'm just passing on the message,' Suzy said, and hung up without identifying herself. Before she got out of the room the telephone began to ring; she paused, looking at it, and knew it had to be Carina ringing up to ask Liam what he meant by cancelling their date at such short notice. Walking back to it, she took it off the hook and left it on the desk, squawking, while she went back to the kitchen. What, she wondered, would Carina do with her duck and cherries?

The doctor arrived just after seven o'clock and

when Suzy took him into the bedroom they found Liam fast asleep, perspiration on his face and his colour no longer so hectic. He woke up, starting, as the doctor bent over him, and Suzy slipped quietly out of the room, closing the door. The doctor rejoined her ten minutes later, smiling.

'Influenza,' he told Suzy cheerfully. 'The worst of it's over now, but keep him in bed for a few days.' Handing her a prescription, he added, 'And see he takes the antibiotics for his throat at the prescribed intervals—it's important that he finishes the treatment or there may be a recurrence. Make sure he has plenty of fluids; he won't feel like eating for a day or so, but when he does make sure he stays on a light diet at first: boiled fish, scrambled eggs, that sort of thing.'

Suzy smiled tightly and showed him out, then stood there staring down at the prescription. She would have to get this to a late-night chemist at once. She looked quietly in at Liam and saw that he had already gone back to sleep, so she let herself out of the flat and went down to the Chinese restaurant. There were a few people eating in it, but the girl came over at once, smiling.

'How Mr Moor?'

'He's got influenza, but the doctor thinks the worst is over.'

'Oh, good! Very glad.'

Suzy smiled back, her eyes wry. 'He isn't a good patient.'

'No. Typical man,' said Ann Ling, her black eyes dancing.

'I have to find a late-night chemist; do you know if there's one around here?'

'Next block, this side of road,' Ann Ling directed, pointing. 'You stay with Mr Moor now?'

'I'll have to see,' said Suzy, leaving with a polite smile. She had been asking herself that question for a long time—should she go and leave Liam alone in this state? Or should she stay at least for tonight? He would sleep until the morning and she could use the couch in his sitting-room, but was it wise? What construction would Liam put on it? He had a cynical mind and he despised her; he would read too much into the fact that she had stayed with him all night.

CHAPTER SEVEN

Suzy woke Liam at ten o'clock to take the medicine the doctor had prescribed. He seemed too sleepy to take in what was happening; his eyes were heavy and drowsy and his body slack as she lifted the spoon to his mouth.

'What's this?' he muttered.

She firmly pushed the spoon between his lips. 'Just swallow it and don't argue.'

He swallowed, grimacing. 'Filthy stuff! Are you poisoning me?'

'No, I'd just like to,' Suzy said coldly, snapping off the bedside lamp and going out. She heard the springs give as he turned over and the long yawn with which he settled down again, then softly she shut the door. She had to give him another dose at four in the morning, so she rang the telephone operator and asked for an alarm call at that hour, then made herself a bed on the couch with a couple of cushions and a spare blanket she had found in the airing cupboard in the bathroom.

When the telephone call woke her she stumbled out of the room and splashed her face with cold water before taking Liam the medicine.

This time she found him awake, his bedside lamp already lit. Suzy stopped in the doorway, frowning.

'Why aren't you asleep? Is something wrong?'

He lay back against the pillows, his jawline stubbled and dark, and considered her with cool curiosity. 'What are you doing here? I woke up when the phone rang, then I heard someone moving about—it's four in the morning, what the hell is going on here?'

Suzy came slowly over to the bed, watching him warily. 'Don't you remember last night? I was here looking after you ...'

'I'm not crazy, of course I remember last night,' he snapped, his dark brows scowling over his distant eyes. 'But why are you still here?'

She held out the bottle and the spoon. 'To make sure you take this!'

He lay silently watching her uncap the bottle and pour some of the amber liquid into the spoon; she held it out and he grimly swallowed the medicine. Suzy put a hand towards the lamp switch and Liam shot his fingers forward to arrest the movement.

'No, leave it on!'

'You should be asleep,' she protested, trying to pull free.

'I was—until the phone rang. Who was ringing at this time of night?'

'The operator; it was an alarm call for me. The doctor said you had to have the medicine every six hours on the dot and I was afraid I wouldn't wake up.'

'You sleep well, do you?' Liam asked with sudden bitterness, and she winced, losing colour.

'Don't start that again!' she said, freeing herself of his grip and turning to the door.

'I don't,' he said. 'I haven't slept well for three years. I keep thinking I've got over it, but it all comes back sooner or later, like a recurring illness, some germ in the blood which can't be cured.'

The bleakness in his voice made it impossible for her to walk out. She turned and looked at him with an ache of the heart. He was pale now, where he had been flushed with fever; the tension in his mind showed in the taut lock of cheekbones and jaw and in those frozen grey eyes.

'You can't change the past by brooding over it,' she said gently. 'It happened, and nothing will alter that. Mark is dead, but you shouldn't blame yourself, because he was as much at fault as either of us; you know that, if you're honest with yourself. Mark's own character made him drive like a maniac that day. He might just as well have been driving on a track and been killed in a race. I was always afraid that that would happen one day.'

'I wanted him dead!' Liam broke out hoarsely, his hands screwed into fists and striking violently on the bed.

Suzy stiffened in shock, staring.

'When he told me you were going to marry him after all, I wanted to kill him, and then he crashed and I felt as if I had!' he grated, trembling.

She went back to him, put down the bottle of medicine and knelt on the bed, shaking him. 'But you didn't kill him! Mark killed himself, and he'd have killed you if he could. He was trying to kill you; why do you think he pushed you into racing along that road with him? Mark was selfish and spoilt; he'd had his own way all his life and he couldn't stand losing— either a race or a woman. When I told him I loved you he went crazy, but he didn't love me; that isn't how love feels. I was just one of his possessions and he wouldn't let go of me without a fight, but he never knew a thing about me because he didn't care enough to find out. All I was to Mark was a flower to wear in his buttonhole, a doll to put on a cushion. I wasn't a person, he didn't love me, and once I realised that I stopped caring about him too.'

Liam lay there staring up at her, his face bloodless and blank. When her husky torrent of words stopped she let go of his shoulders and scrambled off the bed, biting her lower lip.

'Please, try to sleep,' she whispered, switching off the light so that she need no longer see that accusing face. 'You won't get better if you don't sleep.'

'You must go in the morning,' Liam said harshly.

Suzy closed the door without answering, but he hadn't needed to say it. She had every intention of leaving in the morning.

She didn't think she would go back to sleep that night, but towards dawn she drifted into a light doze and then into a deeper sleep and her familiar, bitter dream.

'Suzy! Suzy!' The deep, angry voice dragged her out of the darkness, and she opened her eyes dazedly and looked into Liam's face with a pang of anguish which was worse than anything she had suffered in the dream.

'You were having a nightmare,' Liam said tersely, his hands digging into her bare shoulders.

She closed her eyes again, briefly, struggling with tears and not wanting him to see that.

'I'm sorry I woke you again,' she whispered, trembling.

'I wasn't asleep.' His hands loosened their grip, but instead of letting go of her they slid slowly along her shoulderblades, smoothing her skin. Suzy suddenly remembered that she was only wearing a slip and panties; she had taken off her dress because it was getting creased. Heat ran through her in a volcanic flow.

Without opening her eyes she put her own hands on his wrists and pulled the wandering fingers down, pushing them away.

'How could I sleep, knowing you were in the next room?' Liam asked thickly, sitting down on the couch so that he hemmed her in and made it impossible for her to move.

Her nerves leapt with alarmed fire. 'You must go back to bed. You're still feverish!'

'Yes,' he whispered, bending over her and kissing her neck and her shoulders, his hands holding her down when she tried to escape. His face burrowed between her breasts and she shook violently, her eyes closing in a mixture of pain and pleasure which made her moan softly.

'Please, don't, Liam,' she groaned.

'I'm feverish, I don't know what I'm doing,' he mocked, one hand exploring below the blanket, fondling her hip, her thigh, sliding upward in an intimate movement that made her stomach clench in fierce desire.

'Is that what you want? Is that why you stayed?' he asked, his lips on the soft, warm flesh of her breasts, pushing aside the silk and lace of the slip to expose the hard pink nipples, his tongue gently caressing them until Suzy was almost crazy. She writhed and struggled against the hands holding her down, but Liam would not let her escape yet; he shifted his body and Suzy found his full weight anchoring her, his knee pushing her thighs apart. Panic rose up inside her as she recognised the sensations making havoc inside herself; if she didn't stop him soon she never would, and she would hate herself for letting him make love to her with this mocking contempt.

She went dead, lying there slackly, cold and withdrawn, as he touched her, and Liam realised it after a moment and arched his body to stare down at her.

Suzy stared back, her eyes defiant. 'I can't stop you but I'll despise you if you do it,' she said, and saw his eyes flicker.

'How Victorian!'

'I mean it,' she insisted, her body rigid.

'You want me; do you think I can't feel it?' He cupped one breast, his thumb moving roughly backwards and forwards across the nipple, and Suzy fought not to enjoy the seductive teasing of the friction. Liam's eyes glowed, the pupils enlarged, their glitter tormenting. 'Stop pretending, Suzy,' he whispered. 'We're both adults and we both know it's good between us; we both remember that only too well, don't we? When we made love we touched the sky, even if it was just physical.'

'Was it just physical for you, Liam?' she asked sadly, and saw his face twist in sudden anger.

'This time it would be!'

She looked away, fighting tears. 'That's why I don't want it. I won't be used like that!'

'You're in no position to talk about being used! What else did you do to me?'

'That's not the truth, Liam. I didn't use you. I meant everything I said. It was Mark who lied, not me, but I don't expect you to believe that. You're too busy feeling guilty over his death; it makes it easier for you to bear the memory of what happened if you can blame me.'

She felt him stiffen, his body still pressed close to hers, as if in warm intimacy. Their bodies did not know that they were enemies; their skin clung, their limbs relaxed one against another, happy to merge. If human beings couldn't talk, would they be much happier? Suzy wondered wryly.

'You feel some guilt, too,' he muttered, 'or you wouldn't be having nightmares about it.'

Her eyes leapt to his face and he gave her a crooked smile, nodding. 'You screamed his name,' he added tersely. 'Do you often dream about it, or was this a one-off?'

'I've had a few nightmares,' she admitted, shivering. 'Of course I feel guilty because he died and we didn't, but my rational mind tells me I was no more to blame than Mark himself. I wasn't driving his car—he was. He treated me pretty casually, or have you forgotten that? He pushed me out of sight, made me a secret plaything. He was too scared of his mother to care if he hurt my feelings or my pride. I don't suppose it even occurred to him that it might bother me. Mark didn't love me, Liam. He wasn't capable of loving anyone but himself. His own pleasure, his own wants and needs, were all he cared about, and when I told him I didn't love him any more, that I'd fallen in love with you, he wasn't really hurt. It was just his pride that suffered. You ran off with his toy and he came after you to get it back; that's all that really happened.'

He had listened in silence, his face unreadable; she had no idea what, if anything, he felt as he watched her, but at last he got up and went to the door, pausing there with his head turned back to glance at her. 'Why did you come here?'

'I told you—I rang and you sounded odd, I was worried ...'

His mouth indented, he stared fixedly at her. 'Why did you ring in the first place?'

Suzy bit her lip, running a hand through her dishevelled hair. 'I'm afraid I'm going to have to tell Alex that you and I knew each other before I gave him your book. I thought I ought to warn you in case Alex decided not to buy the film rights, once he knew.'

Liam's brows dragged together. 'Why the hell

should it make any difference to him? What are you talking about?'

'He might feel that I was in some sort of conspiracy with you,' she faltered, and Liam laughed shortly.

'Aren't you making a mountain out of a molehill? He's interested in my book because he likes it. I don't see Alex Stevenson allowing his secretary to pressure him into paying a large sum for the film rights of a book. . .' His voice stopped dead and he narrowed his eyes at her, his jawline clenched.

Suzy stared back, wondering why he was looking like that, and then Liam said icily, 'Unless, of course, he's in love with you.'

Scalding colour hit her face. She sat up, holding the blanket up to her throat, shaking her head angrily. 'Don't be ridiculous, of course he isn't!'

'Then why should he be so shocked to hear that you and I once knew each other years ago?'

The whiplash question made her shrink, still shaking her head. 'You don't understand!' she stammered, and he gave her a bitter little smile.

'Then explain it to me. So far it doesn't make any sense unless you and Stevenson have been having an affair and he let you talk him into buying the rights of my book.'

'You know I didn't have anything to do with it! I didn't even know it was in his mind. When I opened the door and saw you that day at Alex's cottage I was dumbstruck.'

'You still haven't explained why Stevenson would

mind so much when he finds out we knew each other!'

She sighed. 'I didn't think of it at first, but Mrs Jonas said Alex would be angry, he'd suspect I had been conspiring with you and I ought to tell him before he finds out some other way.'

Liam leaned against the door frame, his arms folded and his eyes probing. 'Would you run that past me again? I haven't a clue where Mrs Jonas fits into this mess.'

Suzy stammered out an explanation of her brief talk with Leah Jonas, and Liam gave a wry shrug.

'If Stevenson is that paranoid, you'd better tell him, hadn't you? We're supposed to exchange contracts some time next week, so you haven't got much time.'

She gave him an unhappy glance, her blue eyes wide and pleading. 'Liam, I'm sorry—I hope it doesn't make any difference; I hope he still buys your book. I'd hate to be the cause of your losing that chance.'

He gave her a curt nod and went out without answering, and Suzy lay back, her mind and body cold with misery. She would have given anything to be in his arms again, but not like that; that would have been intolerable. Some things you couldn't live with afterwards; giving yourself to a man who despised you was one of them. If she had surrendered to her own hunger for him, she would have found it hard to forgive herself; her pride would have been irreparably damaged.

She waited half an hour before getting up, then had a shower and dressed.

There was no sound from the bedroom. She didn't know if Liam was awake or asleep and she was disinclined to check to see, so she made some coffee and a slice of toast, although she wasn't at all hungry. She would stay here until ten, when she had to give Liam another dose of the medicine, and then she would leave. He was obviously well on the road to recovery, his temperature right down and his mind more or less back to normal. He was hating her again, anyway; for Liam that was fairly normal.

She was just tidying the sitting-room when the doorbell went. Suzy answered it, expecting to see the Chinese girl, but instead she found herself facing a small, slender woman in her late fifties with silvered dark hair and calm pale blue eyes.

'How is he? We were out until midnight and I only found his message on our answering machine when we were getting ready for bed and it seemed too late to drive all this way then, but we got up bright and early and here I am.'

While she was talking the woman had walked past Suzy and down the hall, speaking in a soft, smiling voice over her shoulder, as though they were old friends. Baffled, Suzy followed her, wondering if she had come to the right address.

'Do you mean Liam?' she asked uncertainly. 'Because if you do, he's asleep and I'm afraid he isn't well enough for visitors ...'

The woman walked into the kitchen, sniffing. 'Do I

smell coffee? Oh, I'd love a cup, is it still hot? You're not Chinese, are you?' Suzy dazedly shook her head and the woman laughed. 'No, of course you're not, I didn't think you were, I merely meant . . . Liam said something about the Chinese in the restaurant being very kind and looking after him, but obviously you're someone else,'

'Yes,' said Suzy, staring. 'And you . . .?'

'I'm his mother, didn't I say? Silly of me, I thought you knew, I suppose.' Mrs Moor began to make fresh coffee as if she was very familiar with the little kitchen. 'Valerie Moor,' she added, turning and smiling, her brows rising enquiringly as she waited for Suzy to give her own name.

The smile vanished as she stammered it out. 'Suzy Froy?' Mrs Moor repeated, frowning. 'What are *you* doing here? I didn't think Liam ever saw you any more.'

Suzy turned pale as she read the hostility in the older woman's eyes; it was clear that Mrs Moor knew something about what had happened. Liam must have confided in his parents, given them the bitter version of her actions which he believed himself.

'I had to ring him,' stammered Suzy, her hands twisting at her sides. 'On business. I work for Alex Stevenson and . . .'

'You work for Mr Stevenson, the film director?' interrupted Mrs Moor, looking stunned.

'Yes. That's why I rang Liam, and I realised he was ill, so I came to see if I could help.'

'You came to see if you could help,' Mrs Moor

repeated slowly, her face as cold as arctic wastes. 'I'd have thought you'd done enough for Liam, wouldn't you?'

The sarcasm left Suzy speechless. Her eyes widened, their dark pupils dilated in pain, then she looked away, pressing her lips together to stop the quiver running through them.

'How long have you been here, anyway?'

Suzy couldn't look at Mrs Moor, or answer her; she felt the hot blood flowing into her face and knew that the other woman was watching her intently and reading her reaction all too accurately.

'Have you been here all night?' asked the icy voice, but Suzy stayed silent, knowing that her very silence was answer enough.

She had often wondered what his parents were like. Three years ago she had been looking forward to meeting them, becoming part of their family, a little nervous because Liam was an only son, like Mark, and Suzy couldn't help being afraid that his mother might be as jealous and possessive as Mark's. Liam had laughed at her qualms and told her that his mother wasn't like that at all; she would make his wife very welcome, she couldn't wait to have grandchildren and was always urging him to get married soon.

Liam had told her that Mrs Moor was still very attractive, although she was fifty-four then, and looked much younger than her real age. He had understated his case; Mrs Moor was strikingly attractive: chic and well-groomed, with an amazingly smooth skin for her age, her blue eyes clear and full of

warmth, her smile impulsive and sweet-tempered—
until she realised who Suzy was, when her manner
froze over, leaving Suzy with a melancholy sense of
what might have been.

Suzy was quite sure that they would have liked each
other if Liam hadn't been a wall between them. She
looked at Liam's mother with an aching heart; her
whole life seemed to be littered with might-have-
beens and regrets for yesterday.

'I don't understand any of this,' Mrs Moor said
tightly, 'but I think you'd better go now, don't you? I
want to talk to Liam and I'd rather not have an
audience.'

Suzy turned away, not looking where she was
going, and walked straight into Liam just outside the
kitchen door. He caught her shoulders and she reeled
away with a gasp.

'What's the matter now?' he asked harshly,
shaking her a little, and then his mother appeared in
the doorway and Liam looked up, startled, his hands
clenching on Suzy for an instant before they released
her.

'I'm sorry we were out last night when you rang,'
Mrs Moor said in a flat voice. 'We found the message
on the machine when we got back and I came at once.
How do you feel? You look haggard, Liam.'

Suzy looked through her lashes at him. His mother
was right; he looked pale and drawn, his black hair
dishevelled and his jaw dark with stubble because he
hadn't shaved for several days. He was still in his
pyjamas but wore a dressing-gown over them.

He gave his mother a rueful smile, shrugging. 'I wasn't expecting you so soon; you must have left at the crack of dawn. There was no need to panic. I'm sorry if I made it sound as if I was at death's door. It's only 'flu, but I felt terrible when I rang you.'

'You shouldn't be out of bed. Get back there!' Mrs Moor scolded, shooing him into the bedroom and closing the door.

Suzy stood in the little hall, staring at the closed door with a set expression. She could guess what Liam's mother was saying to him: demanding to know why Suzy was here and what was going on between them, reminding him of what had happened three years ago—as if he needed any reminders!

She quietly collected her things from the sitting-room and let herself out of the front door without telling them she was leaving. It was simpler that way.

At the corner of the road she managed to get a taxi; she felt the extravagance was justified. She didn't have the energy to walk to the nearest underground station and fight her way on to a train. She wanted to get away from there as quickly as possible; she wanted to get back to her own flat, where she could cry without anyone knowing anything about it.

When Alex and Sara got to London she would have to tell them enough of the truth to make them understand that she certainly had not been conspiring with Liam to sell his book to the film company, and she wasn't looking forward to that interview. It would be a painful experience and she knew that she was going to have to resign from her job afterwards, even if Alex believed her story, because she couldn't bear the idea of working with him while he was making Liam's film. She never wanted to see Liam again. She had to get away from the whole tangle and make a new beginning somewhere.

She stared out of the taxi at the London streets through which they were driving. How did you get away from yourself, though? Wherever you went, you took yourself with you, and with yourself you carried all the emotional luggage you had acquired throughout your life. You couldn't shed any of it, however hard you tried. She had tried hard enough, God knew. It hadn't worked. Fate had pushed it all back at her, mocking her folly.

CHAPTER EIGHT

SUZY was at her desk when Alex walked into the office. Her head lifted and her lips parted in a gasp of surprise. Alex grinned at her, his eyes amused.

'Don't look at me like that! I'm not a ghost. You knew I was going to call in today, didn't you?'

'Yes, but I can't believe how well you look!' she said, laughing as she got to her feet. 'The last time I saw you, I didn't think you'd be fit to work for months, but you really look terrific!'

He had shaken off the lacklustre look, the weariness and pallor which had disturbed her when she saw him down at his cottage just two weeks ago. His eyes were clear and bright, his colour back to normal—this was more like the old, energetic, forceful Alex she had such difficulty keeping up with when he charged through the day like a tank on a battlefield.

'Sara must be happy,' she said. 'Is she with you?'

'In London, yes, but not here now. She went shopping in Bond Street—I couldn't think of an excuse to stop her.' He grinned. 'I'll probably be broke by teatime. She had that spend, spend, spend look.' He prowled around the office, staring at everything as if familiarising himself with it all over again. 'But she deserves a little fun,' he added lightly. 'She had a bad time with me, and you're right, Suzy, she is happy now I'm back on my feet.'

'You're still going away, though, aren't you?' Suzy asked as he picked up a file of letters and flicked over them.

'Yes, I promised Sara I would. That's what she's doing now—buying some clothes to take with her. I got the same old story; she hadn't got a thing to wear on the beach. All you need for a holiday over there is a pair of shorts and a couple of T-shirts; Sara has a drawerful of bikinis, but as soon as we got to London she was eager to get to the shops and buy some more.'

Suzy smiled, but her mind was elsewhere; she was wondering how she was going to tell him about Liam. Alex stopped in front of her desk, surveying her drily.

'You look very pensive; what's on your mind?'

She grimaced. 'You're a mind-reader! I do have something I need to talk about.'

He nodded. 'I wonder if I can guess what it is. Liam Moor?'

Suzy's jaw dropped. 'You knew? *What* do you know?'

'I had a long talk with L.J. on the phone last night—he'd got it from his wife and decided I ought to be told before I signed the contract with Moor.'

Pale, she nodded. 'I know. Mrs Jonas warned me that if I didn't tell you, she would, and I was going to, but . . .'

'Stop quivering like an aspen,' Alex said patiently, giving her a scornful stare. 'What on earth do you think I am? I've never heard such a storm in a teacup in my life! I'm going to say to you what I said to L.J. I decided to buy the rights of Moor's book because it was exactly what I was looking for—I've wanted to make a film around motor-racing for a long time and I liked the love-story angle Moor had woven into his book; I liked the ambiguity of the girl.' He observed Suzy's hard flush with thoughtful eyes. 'I don't want to upset you, Suzy. I frankly don't think of that girl as you. I don't know exactly what happened between you and Moor, but when L.J. suggested that character might be based loosely on you, I simply didn't see it.'

'It isn't me,' muttered Suzy, avoiding his eyes. 'He used some aspects of my character, but that girl isn't me; I wouldn't behave like that.'

'Writers have that prerogative,' Alex said wryly, 'maddening though it may be if we find ourselves being used as a spare part supplier for one of their characters. Perhaps Moor didn't even consciously decide to base the girl on you.'

Suzy didn't comment on that, she was sure Liam had done it very consciously; it had been part of his revenge on her. He had attacked her in print, knowing she couldn't defend herself.

'All this is beside the point. Coming back to L.J.'s concern because you hadn't told me that you once knew Moor, I don't see any reason why you should have told me. You had nothing whatever to do with my decision to buy the rights, and frankly I resent any suggestion that I'm that easily influenced. As I recall it, I didn't even tell you what was in my mind. Before you gave me a copy of the book I'd begun to be interested in it, simply from reading a few reviews. It sounded interesting, a possible basis for a good film script, and once I'd actually read it I was excited by the potential I could see, but you had absolutely nothing to do with it, and I made that crystal clear to L.J.'

Suzy breathed a sigh of relief. 'Well, I knew I hadn't been trying to deceive you, but Mrs Jonas seemed to think . . .'

'Leah doesn't know you as well as I do,' Alex said quite gently. 'Sara and I straightened her out before I came here. Leah has gone shopping with Sara this morning. You can stop looking hunted, Suzy. You have no need to tell me anything and the deal with Moor will go through as arranged.'

She smiled tremulously. 'I'm glad. I wouldn't want to be the cause of Liam losing that chance of having a film; it could make his name.'

'It will make him very rich,' said Alex with dry amusement. 'Quite apart from the money we're paying for the rights, his publishers here and in the States are busy planning a new launch of the book around the time the film is released.' He laughed shortly. 'And I won't even begin shooting the film for at least a year. It's going to be quite a lavish budget, L.J. assures me, and the planning stage will take at least six months, if not longer.'

Suzy nodded, understanding only too well how complex this first stage of making a film could be. Taking a deep breath, she said flatly, 'I shall be resigning, of course, Alex—I feel I must.'

He leaned over her desk, his face impatient. 'Why?'

She was very flushed as he stared at her. Her eyes flickered restlessly away from his searching gaze. 'Well, for various reasons . . .' she stammered.

'Name them. You're a good secretary; I don't want to lose you. Don't you think I have the right to know why you're resigning?'

She couldn't meet his eyes, but sighed. 'They're personal. I'd rather not discuss them.'

Alex walked to and fro in silence for a moment, his hands in his pockets and his head bent. When he stopped in front of her desk again his eyes had an ironic gleam. 'I may take it, I presume, that these reasons have something to do with Liam Moor?'

Suzy's colour deepened. She nodded, her mood very low key.

'Very well,' Alex said calmly. 'I won't accept your resignation now; I'll give you the weekend to consider it. Sara and I will be boarding our cruise ship on Monday afternoon. You can ring me on Monday morning and tell me your decision, and I hope you'll decide to stay, Suzy.'

Leah Jonas rang her late that afternoon, her voice husky and uncertain. 'I have to apologise to you, Suzy. Alex tore a strip off me, both for suspecting for an instant that you and Mr Moor might be in collusion and for daring to imagine that anyone at all could influence Alex Stevenson.'

Suzy laughed. 'I'm glad it's all cleared up, anyway. Please don't worry about it. I did understand why you had some doubts.'

'Alex didn't,' Leah Jonas said wryly. 'I've offended him irretrievably, I'm afraid. I cast aspersions on his absolute independence of mind; the unforgivable sin, I gather.'

'Oh, I'm sure he'll soon get over it. Alex doesn't bear grudges; that's one thing I admire about him. He's quite fair-minded really for an egomaniac.'

Leah chuckled softly. 'You're very comforting! I hope you're right. Tell me, have you ever called Alex an egomaniac to his face?'

'Not in so many words,' Suzy said demurely, and heard the other woman chuckle again.

'When Alex and Sara get back, we plan to throw a party for them—just a few people and a cold buffet at our house, to celebrate Alex's recovery. I hope you'll come.'

Suzy was taken aback; she had never been invited to the Jonases' home before. She had only read about it: stories about its palatial size and extensive walled gardens stocked with rare trees and flowers. The parties Leonard and his wife held were famous; the sort of glamorous affair gossip columns delighted in, and that was as close as Suzy had ever got to a Jonas party—reading about it in a newspaper.

'Thank you, I'd love to,' she said, but did not add that she would no longer be working for the company by the time Alex returned from his convalescence. As she hung up she gave a sigh of regret; she would have loved to be at that party. From what she knew of Mrs Jonas the few people and simple little cold buffet would become a magical event by the time it actually happened.

Leah designed her parties with the same flair she showed in her dress designs; each was quite different, centred on a theme and wildly extravagant. That was what made them so newsworthy, and both L.J. and his wife shrewdly used their parties for publicity purposes. No doubt this one for Alex was intended to trumpet the fact that Empire Films had bought Liam's book and would be making a film of it.

Suzy went back to work with a shrug. Even if she hadn't been resigning, she couldn't have gone to that party if Liam was going to be there. From now on she was going to avoid him like the plague, she reminded herself, until she had given notice and worked her last month with the firm, as her contract stipulated. Alex had given her until Monday to make the final decision, but she didn't need the time—she knew she had to go.

When she left that evening, she found herself in the lift with Joshua, who was in one of his mournful moods and told her he was missing Linda more each day.

'Why don't you take a week off and fly over to Spain to see her?' Suzy suggested, impatient with his helpless brooding. 'It should be lovely over there at this time of the year; spring is always the best time to visit the Mediterranean countries.'

Joshua looked uncertain. 'I did hear rumours that Linda was buzzing around with one of the technicians over there,' he complained. 'If I turn up out of the blue she might not be pleased to see me.'

Suzy eyed him incredulously. 'If you really think Linda's going out with someone else, why mope over her? Honestly, Joshua, you need your head examined!'

'I'm not exactly a prize in life's lottery,' he sighed. 'Are you doing anything this weekend, Suzy?'

She said firmly that she was very busy and hurried away to the underground station to get her train. At times she wondered if it was Linda who deserved sympathy, not Joshua; he seemed to clutch his lovesick state like a security blanket, and perhaps if Linda actually suggested they got married Joshua would flee like a hunted deer. Was he more in love with being unhappy than he was with Linda?

She wasn't babysitting for Clarrie that weekend because her sister was taking the children to visit their grandparents in Wales. Derek's parents lived in an old flint and slate cottage in the Brecon Beacons, one of the most beautiful areas of Wales. From the windows of the little cottage you got some incredible views of that landscape, but it wasn't the beauty of the scenery that the little boys loved. They adored visiting their grandparents because they were allowed to help out with the chores, something they rarely did at home. Derek's parents bred goats and sold goat's milk, yoghurt and cheese. They were up at first light and busy around their smallholding, so when Clarrie's boys stayed there they got up too, and fed goats and hens, collected eggs from the nesting boxes, helped to churn and pack cheese, helped their grandfather to repair the drystone walls which surrounded the property and after all that activity in the wine-sharp air came back indoors to eat vast meals.

'I wouldn't mind, but if I asked them to help me wash up they would vanish pronto,' Clarrie always complained, but she looked forward to those week-ends too, because while her children were kept busy she could go for walks with Derek or curl up in a chair with a book until it was time to feed Anna. Clarrie got on well with her mother-in-law, particularly as they lived so far apart and only saw each other at long intervals. The visits were always happy ones for the whole family.

Suzy had the whole weekend to herself and enjoyed it in her own way, spending Saturday shopping and doing the housework in the morning and in the afternoon having a lengthy beauty treatment in a salon in the next street. She had her ash-blonde hair re-styled in a bubbly cluster of curls, had a facial massage and a manicure. It was all very relaxing and she wasn't required to think; she merely lay back in a chair and closed her eyes, emptying her head, especially of thoughts of Liam. That evening she went to see a musical comedy show in the West End with some friends. The show ended at half past ten and they all went to have supper at an Italian restaurant nearby. It was one in the morning before Suzy got home and two before she got to sleep. She slept late on the Sunday morning, and was just having some black coffee and an apple for a belated breakfast when someone rang the doorbell.

As she opened the door she had a premonitory qualm and it wasn't really a surprise to find Liam standing there.

'We don't have anything to say,' Suzy said tightly, blocking his entry.

'You may not!' he drawled, advancing. 'I do.'

'I don't want to listen, whatever it is!' she snapped, but she hesitated to try to stop him pushing past her. She knew she wouldn't win a physical confrontation;

Liam had too many weapons and she was feeling distinctly frail after her late night.

He calmly walked past into the kitchen, saying over his shoulder, 'First of all, I have to thank you for taking such care of me when I was ill.'

'Oh,' she said, surprised, as she shut the front door and followed him. 'That's OK. Anyone would have done the same.'

He leaned casually against the table, his arms folded, smiling at her. Suzy's heart constricted and she felt her colour change. He looked far too sexy in the dark grey trousers and white cashmere sweater; her eyes flickered restlessly over him with a helpless yearning she couldn't control. She really had to stop caring about him; she was behaving like a fool. When would she learn?

'I wasn't an easy patient, I'm afraid,' he murmured wryly, 'I was delirious half the time, I think.'

Suzy lowered her eyes, aware that she was blushing like a schoolgirl. Was he making an oblique apology for having tried to make love to her? In a way, that wasn't so complimentary if what he was trying to say was that he had only made a pass at her because he was delirious, but Liam seemed slightly less hostile than he had been since they met again, so she half-smiled, shrugging.

'You weren't that much trouble.'

'How very ambiguous!' he drawled, and she laughed huskily.

'Do you want some coffee?'

'Thank you,' he said, his tone dry as if he knew that she was deliberately changing the subject. She handed him the cup and sat down at the kitchen table to finish her own coffee. Liam took another chair and sat down with his lean body casually stretched out inches away from her.

'Why have you given Stevenson your notice?' he asked, and she almost choked on her coffee. Why on earth had Alex told him that?

'Private reasons,' she countered, putting down her cup.

'You're leaving because you don't want to work with me?' he suggested, and she kept her eyes lowered and didn't answer him.

'I got the impression you loved the job,' murmured Liam, his eyes narrowed on her averted face. 'I asked Stevenson if he wanted you to go and he said it would make his life very difficult, you were a first-class secretary and he relied on you.'

'That was nice of him!' Suzy said, surprised but very pleased. Alex didn't hand out compliments like confetti. It was rare for him to praise you for doing your job; he expected the best and only an unusual effort brought a compliment from him.

'You don't want to make his life difficult, do you?' murmured Liam.

'No, but all the same, I really must leave,' she said with stubborn insistence.

'Perhaps you want to make *my* life difficult?'

She gave him an incredulous look. 'How will I do that?'

'By annoying Stevenson. He was obviously very put out because you said you were going and he blames me.'

Suzy bristled at his air of plaintive complaint. 'Well? You know I'm leaving because you've made it impossible for me to stay.'

'How have I done that?' he queried, raising one eyebrow in innocent bewilderment.

Suzy was wordless. She stared at him, dying to slap that bland expression off his face. When she could speak, she stuttered: 'Y-y-you know very well how! You won't let me forget what happened three years ago. Every time I see you we have another bitter argument about it, and I'm sick of carrying your share of the guilt as well as my own. I've got to get away from you, and I hope you're pleased with yourself for wrecking my life for the second time!'

Liam put down his cup and got up, wandering over to the window to stare out over the quiet London street. 'I'm not,' he said quietly with his back to her.

Suzy kept very still, watching him, her eyes on the way his dark hair tapered into his nape, on the long, graceful line of his spine in the clinging cashmere sweater, his smooth hips and long legs. She was afraid this was another game, another trap for her. She wasn't prepared to react to it until she knew exactly what Liam was up to.

'Three years ago you didn't come to see me in that hospital and when I realised you weren't coming I became very bitter,' he told her. 'I began to believe what Mark had told me, and I hated you for the fool I'd been. I hated you because Mark was dead and I felt so damned guilty—it was so easy to put all the blame on you; it made it bearable for me at first. You're right about that. I did make you the scapegoat for the whole miserable mess, and I've spent the last three years brooding over what happened. When I saw you again, my first impulse was to want to hurt you the way I'd been hurt. I had a lot of poison stored up inside me; I had to let it out, it had festered in me for years. I wasn't ready to listen to anything you said; I just hit out at you and went on hitting in every way I could. No holds barred.'

He paused, breathing roughly, and Suzy felt a tremor of pain run through her as she guessed what he was thinking. He had made love to her ruthlessly to hurt her; that was the real cruelty of what he had done.

Liam turned slowly and she couldn't meet his eyes; she didn't want him to read the full extent of the damage he had done to her pride and her heart.

'Eventually, I did start to listen,' he said flatly. 'I started thinking, too. I was able to be rational once I'd got rid of all that poison. I believe you, Suzy. If Mark hadn't been killed I would never have believed his version, I knew him better than anyone else ever did. Mark *was* spoilt and selfish, and he'd inherited a possessive streak from his mother.' He drew in his lip, his teeth clenched on it, shrugging, then sighed and said, 'This isn't easy for me to say—but I'm sorry.' His voice was husky, not quite steady. 'I know I've behaved unforgivably and I'm not asking you to forgive me, but I am asking you not to resign. I've done you enough harm already; I don't want to smash up your life again. If you really can't face seeing me, I'll refuse to sign the contract and there won't be a film, but whatever happens, I can't let you leave your job over me.'

Suzy met his eyes briefly and then looked away. 'I don't want you to miss the chance of having your book made into a film,' she whispered.

'That doesn't matter a damn!' Liam said impatiently. 'You mustn't resign; promise me you won't. If you need an assurance that I won't make any more trouble for you, you have it. You'll never hear another word from me about Mark or what happened between us—that's all over. We'll forget we ever met before, we'll meet as strangers from now on, polite strangers. You can feel quite safe if you stay in your job, Suzy.'

She listened with lowered eyes; his voice was low and cool and very firm. She did not doubt that he meant what he said. She could withdraw her notice and stay in her job without worrying about Liam. She knew him well enough to trust his word, and her spirits ought to have risen; she should be lightheaded with relief, but she wasn't. She was aching with an intolerable sense of longing because what Liam was saying was that, in putting the past behind him and forgetting it, he was completely over her. It was Suzy he meant to forget. He intended that they should become strangers in future; when they did meet it would be a distant courtesy she would receive from him instead of the angry contempt and reluctant desire he had shown her in his flat, and if she had any sense she would be glad about that.

Why, then, wasn't she? Why did she feel like crying? Suzy asked herself the rhetorical question endlessly after Liam had gone and she was alone. Of course, she knew the answer, but she wished she didn't. If Liam could forget they had ever met, if he could think about her as if she were a stranger, then why couldn't she do the same?

Why couldn't she be wise and stop loving him?

CHAPTER NINE

SHE rang Alex early on the Monday morning to tell him that she would not be resigning. He didn't waste much time on being pleased to hear this, just said briskly, 'At least you're talking sense now. Have you got a pad and pen? Right, while I'm away I shall want ...'

Suzy scribbled rapid shorthand notes, her expression wry. What had she expected? Flags and the national anthem? Alex was not the type. If she had left, he would have shrugged and found himself a replacement. Nobody is indispensable.

'I don't want you getting bored while I'm not here,' he said genially, and she pulled faces, grateful that he could not see her. 'So I've told Liam he can borrow you if he needs a typist—apparently he can only type with two fingers. We'll need half a dozen copies for a script conference when I get back. Make sure he's knocked out something or other, will you, Suzy? It will probably be completely hopeless, but it will give us something to work with.'

Appalled, she began to stammer a protest. 'But Alex, I can't ...'

Blandly, he cut through the husky words. 'I must go, Suzy—Sara's waiting for me. See you when we get back. Have fun!'

Suzy heard the phone click and wanted to scream.

Alex couldn't do this to her. She put the phone down and stared at it like someone watching a snake which has just bitten them. What did he mean, have fun? Was he completely insensitive?

That was a stupid question. Of course he was! When his own interests clashed with those of anybody else, Alex simply railroaded them. If he realised that she wouldn't be too eager to work with Liam he would simply shrug and say, 'Too bad, get on with it. What do you think you're paid for? Just do your job and stop complaining.'

He was right, Suzy told herself without any real conviction. Hadn't Liam said that from now on they would be polite strangers if they met? She would shortly be finding out whether or not he had meant that.

She was on edge for the next few days, but by Wednesday afternoon she had stopped expecting Liam to ring or walk into the office. He hadn't put in an appearance, so presumably he had decided not to take up Alex's offer of secretarial help.

As he was working with Carina, of course, he wouldn't need a typist, she suddenly realised—why had Alex thought otherwise? He must have forgotten that Carina had been a secretary at the very start of her career, when she first left college. Carina was clever, as clever as a zoo full of monkeys; she had a good degree, but she had taken the precaution of acquiring secretarial skills too, and it had paid off, because she had got a job in a script department at Empire Films and within a very short time she had been on her way up the ladder. Some famous men had been the rungs she used. She had soon known a lot of influential people in the film world, but outside that magic circle she was still unknown. The public had never heard of her, and Suzy knew that Carina resented that; she made no secret of her ambition to become a famous name, a household name. She had the ambition and drive to get to the top, if not the creativity, the original talent, but then other very successful people had lacked that and still managed to become famous. Perhaps Carina would make it.

Was Liam to be her next rung? Suzy brooded over that, alone in her flat, wondering if theirs was a purely working relationship or if they had already gone a stage further. If Liam's film was a big success, Carina would grab as much of the limelight as she could, ruthlessly using any emotional hold over Liam she had acquired, but Suzy certainly couldn't warn Liam about that. She wasn't going to sound like a jealous woman.

She would soon start picking up rumours on the grapevine, if Carina was having an affair with Liam. Suzy had no close friends at Empire Films, she hadn't worked there long enough, but she sometimes had lunch with one or two of the other secretaries, or chatted to them in the cloakroom, and they had great fun gossiping about the people they worked with or for. This was a hothouse atmosphere; the film world was a 'people industry' and what was happening in a private life could well have a drastic repercussion for everyone else, so people talked endlessly and avidly.

Suzy didn't think she could bear listening to talk of Liam and Carina; she was in no hurry to find out if her suspicions were correct.

The next morning she heard in the cloakroom that Linda Black had had an accident in Spain; she had tripped over out on location and broken a leg and would be flying home while a replacement was flown out to take her place on the production.

Suzy wondered if Joshua had heard, so she hurried back to her office and rang him, but he was in a meeting. She left a message asking him to get in touch with her when he was free.

'He's having lunch with someone—is this urgent?'asked the gum-chewing girl who had answered the phone, and Suzy said drily that it was quite important, yes. Joshua would undoubtedly think so, anyway; if Linda was in a depressed state of mind after losing her production, she was going to need comfort and Joshua would be eager to offer it. This might be the break Joshua needed—if he really cared about Linda and if she felt anything for him, this was his big chance.

Putting down the phone, she got on with sorting out the latest batch of letters, dealing with all those which didn't need a personal response from Alex, and putting the others into the large file of letters he would have to deal with when he got back. It was already very fat, although she had managed to whittle it down during the week before Alex and Sara left for the Bahamas.

The telephone kept ringing over the next hour and Suzy's computer had developed temporary amnesia and kept refusing to give back what she had just fed into it. She thought of going to lunch early to give it time to cure itself, but when she looked at the windows she found them streaked with rain, and decided she should stay in her office, anyway, until she got a chance to talk to Joshua.

Even as she thought that, the door opened and he shot in, his face distracted. 'What's so urgent?' he demanded, and Suzy quickly gave him the news about Linda.

'A broken leg?' Joshua sat down on the edge of her desk, slightly reassured. 'My God, when I got your message I knew it had to be something about Linda and I imagined the worst . . . are you sure that's all? Just a broken leg?'

'Isn't it bad enough, poor Linda?' Suzy asked wryly. 'I should think she's sick as hell about leaving the production and having to come home.'

'I bet she is,' Joshua agreed. 'They're working on a very tight schedule—even a day's delay could cost a fortune or Linda would probably have tried to talk them into letting her carry on as soon as she was over the worst. When does she get back? I could meet the plane.'

'You'll have to get that from L.J.'s office. I heard it from one of the typists in the cloakroom, but she only knew what had happened because she overheard Madeleine Bentley talking on the phone. She didn't know any details.'

'I'll pop down and chat Madeleine Bentley up, then,' Joshua decided cheerfully, running a hand over his hair and straightening his tie.

Suzy suppressed a smile and he noticed the amusement in her face, saying, 'Don't laugh at me,

Suzy! I need all my self-confidence! I'm trying to nerve myself up to proposing.'

'To Madeleine?' She opened her eyes wide in mock amazement.

He gave a croak of laughter. 'You know I meant Linda! Don't tease.' He took Suzy's hand and held it tightly. 'Do you think I've any chance with her?'

'Joshua, how could I possibly know that?' said Suzy, feeling sorry for him.

'You're a woman, you must understand Linda better than I do. Just tell me, do you think I should risk it? If she says no this time I'll have to stop seeing her; I can't go on like this.'

Suzy looked at him ruefully, and he sighed.

'All I want to know is, have I got a chance?'

While she was considering her reply to that, the door opened and Liam walked in and stopped dead, staring. Joshua went crimson and stood up, muttering, 'Well, I'll see you later,' to Suzy.

'Yes,' she said huskily, eyes lowered, but through her lashes she watched Liam move out of the way to let Joshua pass and saw the blankness of Liam's expression as well as the irritated hunch of Joshua's shoulders as he walked past. They didn't speak to each other, and when the other man had gone Liam closed the door quietly and turned to face her with distant courtesy.

'Sorry to barge in like that,' he said, and didn't wait for Suzy's answer before going on. 'Alex Stevenson told me you might be prepared to do some typing for me. I hope it isn't too much of an imposition.'

'No, of course not,' Suzy stammered.

Liam laid a folder on the desk. 'I've handwritten the first thirty pages. Would you mind glancing through it to make sure you can read my scribble?'

Suzy fumbled nervously as she picked up the folder and opened it, and some pages floated to the floor. Shakily, she knelt down to pick them up. Liam knelt down too, and as she leant forward so did he. Their heads banged; she gave a little gasp and shot to her feet, trembling like a leaf. Liam silently picked up the sheets and handed them to her without comment.

She found it hard to focus on the uneven lines of writing, and even when she stopped seeing through a faint haze the words didn't make much sense. Liam's handwriting was a black scrawl: very personal, very individual and impossible to read.

'Having trouble?' He sounded rueful. 'I thought you might. I wrote it rather fast.'

Suzy looked up and was startled to find him nearer than she had expected. He was wearing casual clothes today: a black polo-neck sweater, black cords. The physical impact of his presence made her intensely nervous.

'I expect I'll get used to it,' she said dubiously. 'I'm sorry but I'm going to need a little help in deciphering this line.' She pointed to one particularly badly written passage and Liam slid off the desk and picked up the chair on the other side of it, bringing it round next to her. He sat down, his knee briefly touching hers.

'Show me.' He stared at the words she indicated, frowning. 'Hell! Oh, yes, that's a t, not an l. I forgot to cross it.' He sighed and ran his eye down the page.

'Sorry about this, but—look, it might be quicker if I dictated it to you.'

'Now?' Suzy frowned, and Liam watched her through his lashes.

'Isn't that convenient? Got a date?' He ran his eyes down over her, noticing every detail of the way she had carefully brushed her hair, applied her make-up, put on a very pretty coral-pink dress. 'I thought you looked very chic,' he said, and Suzy blushed.

'I could ...' The phone began to ring and she jumped, the tinny sound sharply intrusive in her nervous state. 'Sorry, excuse me,' she stammered to Liam, and picked up the phone. While she was talking and making shorthand notes of what was said on the other end of the line, Liam prowled about restlessly, and Suzy tried to keep track of him without letting him know that she was watching him. Having him in her office was like having a tiger there; it made it impossible to relax or think of anything else. Her nerves were at taut stretch the whole time.

Once she caught a look from behind his lowered lashes, a secretive, rapid glance which warned her that he did know she kept looking at him. She forced herself to look down at her notepad after that.

A moment later, putting the phone down, she said huskily, 'Sorry, where were we? Oh, yes. If you do want to dictate, the afternoons would be easiest for me. I have a lot of routine work to get through in the mornings, so I couldn't work then, I'm afraid, but while Alex is away there isn't much to do after lunch.'

'Afternoons, then,' he said. 'Here?'

The door opened and one of the other secretaries

walked in, gave Liam an interested glance, and said to Suzy, 'Have you got the file on Ralynsky which Mr Stevenson borrowed from Hector?'

Suzy pushed back her chair and got up, crossing the room quickly to hunt through the row of thick files on top of one of the cabinets. Ralynsky was a temperamental composer who sometimes wrote brilliant film music. Other times he signed a contract and then didn't come up with anything for months.

She turned, the file in her hand, and gave it to the waiting girl, who smiled sweetly at Liam as she muttered, 'Thanks,' to Suzy. 'Sorry to interrupt,' she told Liam. 'Are you standing in for Mr Stevenson while he's away? I'm Jill, by the way—I work for Hector Williams.'

Liam smiled back, his eyes gleaming as they ran over her. She got that sort of look from most of the men in the building. Jill was pretty and very sure of herself; she dimpled at Liam's glance, waiting for him to introduce himself, which, of course, he did promptly enough.

'The racing driver!' exclaimed Jill, her smile widening. 'I'd heard that we might be making your book into a film—I can't wait to see it. Are you working with Suzy on the script? Lucky Suzy.'

'Thank you,' Liam said blandly, smiling, and Suzy gritted her teeth. Jill gave her a teasing look.

'Wait till Joshua hears about this! He isn't going to like it!'

She went out chuckling, and Liam coolly considered Suzy's flushed and angry face.

'Isn't he?' he enquired without appearing to care

much either way. 'Everyone seems to know about it—
you'd better give him his answer pretty soon before
you find yourself faced with a fait accompli.'

Baffled, Suzy stared. 'What are you talking about?'

'He was proposing when I came in just now, wasn't
he?' He mercilessly watched her face as she stiffened
in shock and incredulity. 'Are you going to accept?
I'd think twice, Suzy. In fact, I'd think very hard for
a long time, if I were you. He may be a nice enough
guy, but he isn't in your class; you'd run rings round
him, and I don't think a woman's ever happy with a
husband she can't respect.'

Suzy was too stunned to answer for a moment, and
then the phone rang again, and she gratefully ran to
answer it. By the time she put the phone down Liam
was gathering up the pages of his script, frowning
impatiently.

'This isn't going to work!' he told her brusquely,
and her heart dive-bombed. What did he mean by
that? Couldn't he stand being in the same room with
her? Was his hostility still too strong? She had
dreaded seeing him again, yet she knew that, however
painful it was to be with him and know that they were
divided by an unbridgeable gulf, it would be far worse
never to see him at all.

'I ... I'm sorry ...' she stammered, all her colour
gone.

'Don't apologise!' Liam burst out, frowning
blackly. 'It isn't your fault! But if we worked here, I
can see we'd be permanently interrupted. I've only
been here fifteen minutes, and you've had two visitors
and two phone calls. At that rate, we'd be lucky to get

a page an hour done.'

'Oh,' said Suzy, swallowing in relief. 'Well, I might be able to find another office in the building, but . . .'

'I have a better idea,' Liam said, looking at his watch. 'It's gone one—come and have lunch and we'll discuss my alternative.'

Suzy gazed at him, her mind in a state of confusion. She had to pull herself together. If Liam could be calm and collected, so could she, surely?

He took her coat off its hanger and held it out for her, and she slipped her arms into the sleeves after fumbling slightly. Instead of moving away Liam began straightening the coat collar, his fingers brushing her nape, and warm colour flowed up her face.

This was not going to be easy: working with him; being with him; occasionally, as just now, feeling him touch her—these casual brushes of his fingers might mean nothing to him, but each time Suzy felt her nerves flicker and her throat go dry.

She took a step away jerkily. 'We'd better hurry or they'll have stopped serving lunch by the time we get there,' she muttered, opening the office door.

Outside the building, she instinctively turned towards the little restaurant where she usually ate; it was cheap and the food was reasonable. Liam, however, flagged down a taxi which had just deposited someone a few yards down the road, and, taking Suzy's elbow, summarily assisted her into the back of the cab, telling the driver to take them to Baker Street.

'I know a very good restaurant there,' he explained as Suzy gave him a startled glance.

'If they're good, we probably won't get a table at such short notice!'

'We will,' he said with cool self-confidence, smiling at her in a way that made her eyes dilate. That smile threw her back three years, reminded her of Liam's teasing warmth before they fell in love, sharply emphasised for her just what she had lost, what she would never have again. There would never be another man for her; anyone else would just be second-best. Liam was so special.

'I know the owner,' he was saying. 'In fact, he's a cousin of mine—a cousin several times removed, but a nice guy; you'll like him. He's been living abroad for years, but he decided to settle back here to be close to his mother, who's very old. Henry's an only child, like me. We both suffer from our mothers.' He grinned wryly at her and Suzy winced, remembering the hostility with which his mother had stared at her.

'What's wrong?' asked Liam, his brows a jagged line above his eyes.

'I met your mother at your flat, when you were ill,' she said, with apparent irrelevance. 'I always wondered what she was like ...'

He was silent, watching her in that frowning way, then said flatly, 'I'm sorry if she wasn't very friendly, but ...'

'She took her tone from you,' Suzy finished for him quietly.

'Yes, I suppose that just about sums it up,' he accepted. 'My mother is on my side, always was, always will be, right or wrong—she's that sort of mother. I'll try to give her a different angle on things next time I talk to her. Next time you see her, she won't be quite so cool.'

Cool didn't quite describe the way Mrs Moor had spoken to her and looked at her. It made Suzy miserable to remember the other woman's contemptuous eyes.

The taxi pulled up outside a small restaurant with a faintly Moorish décor: white arches above the plate-glass windows, a sweeping archway above the front door. The name Moor's Restaurant was above the window, painted in imitation of Arabic writing.

The place was crowded, but as they walked in a harassed-looking man in a white suit turned round and saw them and came over to clap Liam on the shoulder.

'Why didn't you ring first, you old idiot? I told you, ring and let me know you're coming.' He ran an eye over the occupied tables, grimacing. 'Well, we'll find you somewhere soon—come and have a drink at the bar while I arrange it.' His smiling black eyes moved on to Suzy. 'Aren't you going to introduce us?' he asked Liam, who grinned wryly at him.

'I suppose I must, although it goes against the grain. I still remember the girl I introduced to you at a party who promptly dropped me and went out with you instead.'

'My God, Liam, that was nearly twenty years ago! You bear your grudges for a long time.' Henry Moor was more or less the same age as Liam, but very tall and thin, his skin so sallow that he looked as if he hadn't shaved, his hair as black as his eyes and his features faintly lugubrious. When Liam introduced Suzy and she offered her hand, Henry held it, looking into her eyes almost hypnotically.

'Suzy,' he repeated. 'Charming name for a charming girl.'

'His intentions are suspect,' Liam said drily. 'Don't trust him an inch, Suzy.'

'All lies,' protested Henry. 'What's a nice girl like you doing out with a guy like him, Suzy? Let me give you my phone number, or can I have yours?'

'Cut the chat,' said Liam with a hard smile. 'And get us this drink, Henry. And some menus—we might as well order while we wait.'

'He has no soul,' Henry told Suzy, ushering them into the little bar adjoining the restaurant. She sank down into one of the deeply upholstered red velvet couches and Liam sat next to her, his proximity seriously disturbing her as she pretended to read the menu while Henry brought them the drinks they had ordered.

'Now, what are you going to have, Suzy?' asked Henry, his pencil poised over a pad, and he nodded approval when she chose the chicken and lemon soup followed by a seafood salad. 'Perfect choice,' he said. 'What sort of job do you do, Suzy?'

'I'm a secretary,' she said, smiling at him.

'Mine, at present,' Liam added tersely. 'And we're having a working lunch, Henry, so take our order and shove off, there's a good chap.'

'He always was a possessive swine,' Henry told Suzy, who was very flushed by now. 'Take no notice

of him, Suzy. What beautiful blue eyes you've got—
there's something about blue-eyed blondes that gets
most men. Look at the Hitchcock films; he always
had an icy blonde in his films. Cool, distant,
mysterious . . .' He grinned at her. 'He'd have loved
you!'

Suzy shuddered, thinking of the Hitchcock films
she had seen. 'Something ghastly usually happened to
the girls in his films, though! He had a very macabre
imagination, especially where blondes were
concerned.'

'Are you a film buff?' asked Henry, and she
nodded. 'So am I,' he said with enthusiasm. 'We must
see a film together some time.'

'If you don't give our order to your kitchen soon,
we won't get any lunch,' Liam interrupted, frowning, and Henry departed, laughing.

'He's very friendly,' Suzy said with a sideways look
at Liam's irritated expression, a nervous pulse
fluttering in her neck at the very idea that Liam
might be jealous. Was Henry right?

'He's a flirt,' Liam said curtly, 'and he likes to
needle me if he can; he's always been the same. If he
sees me with a girl, he always makes a play for her,
just to annoy me.'

Suzy frowned, recognising that it was true, and
reminded at once of Mark. What was there about
Liam that brought out the competitive streak in other
men? Even Joshua seemed to get belligerent whenever he saw him. Was it Liam's own very male
belligerence? Did the competition start with him, or
did his nature make other men bristle and feel

compelled to challenge him?

'I suppose it started when we were kids,' said Liam, oblivious to what she was thinking. 'Little boys are always trying to beat each other at something, and Henry hasn't really grown up.'

Seeing Henry coming over to tell them that their table was now ready, Liam added the last sentence deliberately so that his cousin could hear him, and Henry made a horrible face at him.

'I heard that!'

'You were meant to!'

Henry eyed him, grinning. 'Who did you say hadn't grown up?' He quickly looked at Suzy. 'Your table's ready.'

She got up and Henry walked beside her, talking lightly about films. He hadn't exaggerated when he called himself a film buff; he clearly knew an enormous amount about cinema, and Suzy listened with interest, not telling him that she worked for Alex Stevenson because she sensed that Liam did not want to arouse his cousin's curiosity, and probably hadn't yet told him that it was on the cards that his novel was going to be made into a film.

'Enjoy your meal,' he said as a waiter brought them their first course, a steaming tureen of fragrant lemony-scented soup. Henry moved away and Suzy took a spoonful of soup; it was as delicious as it smelt.

'You haven't told Henry that Alex wants to make a film of your book?' she asked Liam, who shook his head.

'He'd never give me any peace.' He leaned over the table, lowering his voice. 'Talking about work, how would you feel about coming over to my flat to take this dictation?'

Suzy stiffened. 'Your flat?' She had such vivid and disturbing memories of the hours she had spent there when he was ill. As they came into her mind she felt her skin heat and her eyes hurriedly dropped to the tablecloth as though she was suddenly fascinated by the golden soup.

'Would you object?'

She struggled to look calm. 'I . . . If it suits you . . .'

'At least we wouldn't get interruptions. I'd pay your expenses, of course—taxi fares, for instance. It would save time if you took a taxi there and back. When could you start?'

'Tomorrow?' she said huskily, wishing she didn't have butterflies in her stomach at the very idea of working alone with him in his flat.

'Good,' he said. 'Don't let this terrific soup get cold. I must say, Henry's got a good chef working for him.'

The rest of the meal was as good as the soup, and the wine served with it helped Suzy to relax more so that she could talk to Liam without that prickling, nervy awareness. He kept their conversation light, asking about her family, telling her what he had done over the last three years, places he had visited, how he had finally got down to writing his book.

'I suppose the hardest part was actually making myself start it,' he said wryly. 'I'd been saying I was going to write for years, but I always had great excuses for putting it off. I was afraid that if I had a shot and failed, I'd never dare to try again, but luckily that didn't happen. Once I'd sat down and begun to write, the story took hold of me.'

Suzy sipped the tiny cup of very strong, very sweet coffee with which they had just been served, her eyes lowered and a bitter irony filling them. Liam had found it easy to write his book because he was writing out his hatred of her, and here she sat, listening to him in these civilised surroundings, drinking coffee calmly as though the book had nothing to do with her. Life was so strange; was he aware of that? While he talked she got the feeling that Liam had almost forgotten how very personally she must be involved with his book.

Henry showed them to the door not long after that, saying teasingly, 'Come again soon, Suzy, and don't bring that guy with you next time.'

'You really ask for it, don't you?' Liam said impatiently. 'One day some guy is going to give you the punch on the nose you deserve.'

Suzy wryly wished he could just let it go, walk away ignoring his cousin's needling, but then she didn't understand what had made Mark and Liam compete, any more than she understood why men were so agressive over things that really didn't matter. Who cared whether you won or lost a race, a game or an argument? The things they clashed over were so unimportant, yet they took it all so seriously!

A taxi was waiting at the kerb. Liam insisted on taking her back to her office before going on to his own flat. 'Tomorrow afternoon at two o'clock, then?' he said as she got out in Wardour Street, and she nodded, hoping she looked calmer than she felt. She

did not want him to know how much of an ordeal it
was going to be for her. Liam had promised that in
future they would meet as strangers, but how could
they ever do that? So much emotion, so much need,
so many hours, days, months and years of her life had
gone into loving him. Had it all been poured uselessly
into the sand? The waste of it made her want to cry.

The following day was warm and sunny. Suzy's
spirits rose as she took a taxi to Liam's flat, arriving
punctually at two. He had cleared a desk for her beside
the window; a typewriter was in position with a new
box of typing paper next to it. It wouldn't be
necessary for her to make carbon copies because she
would be photocopying the script back at the office
later, so that there would be enough copies for
everyone concerned to see the script before Alex
started work on changing it. Did Liam realise how
much more work lay ahead of him? she wondered,
watching his profile as she sat down at the desk and
fed some paper into the typewriter. She had seen
other writers tearing their hair out as it dawned on
them that they would be lucky if one word in a
hundred ended up in the final script.

'I thought we'd start work at once,' Liam said
politely. 'Then we could get a few pages done before
we break to have tea. I don't want to slave-drive, so let
me know if I'm going too fast for you.'

'I'm used to slave-drivers,' she told him with a wry
smile. 'I work for Alex, remember!' Alex was never in
the least worried about forcing the pace of work; she
kept up or else!

She had been so occupied with anxiety about working with Liam alone that she had almost forgotten what the script was about. As he began dictating, she remembered—with a blinding rush of painful feeling she couldn't disguise from him. Her colour went, her skin grew icy, her fingers clumsily hit the wrong keys. That first scene brought back too many memories of the day she had first met Liam. He hadn't invented anything—she heard Mark speaking in his own voice, herself saying words she recalled saying, Liam answering as he had.

She felt Liam watching her as she broke off typing. Silently, he walked away to the other side of the room while she corrected the mistakes she had made. He pulled a book from the shelves and flicked over the pages, his back to her. When he did speak his voice made her jump and stiffen.

'I know this isn't easy for you,' he grated. 'It was Alex's idea, not mine, but now we've started . . . can't you just forget it means anything? It's just a string of words, another script by someone you don't know. Forget it was ever personal.'

'But it is,' she said, her eyes on the page in her typewriter.

'It was once!' he corrected. 'Not any more. I've written it all out, it's gone—I told you, it left a poison in my veins I had to get rid of. For centuries the medical profession used to bleed patients, whatever was wrong with them—they thought it could cure anything, to open the veins. The poison all seeped out with your blood. That may have been a crazy theory, but writing works much better. Once I'd written my

book, it no longer nagged away at me. This is just a
story about people I once knew, Suzy.'

'That wasn't the impression I got when I opened
the door to you when you came to Alex's cottage,' she
muttered, head still bent.

'I hadn't realised I was cured then,' he said wryly.
'Hating can be a habit.'

She flinched, biting her lower lip. Loving could be
a habit, too, and a far more painful one, especially
when you were in love with someone who coolly
admitted that they hated you, even when they put it
in the past tense. She and Liam had moved through
such wild spirals of feeling ever since they met; loving
and hating were mirror images of each other, sharing
an extreme of emotion with only a very fine line
dividing them. It left Suzy drained and cold to know
he no longer felt either love or hate, only a quiet,
polite indifference.

'I'm sorry, Suzy,' he said flatly, watching her. 'If
you don't want to go on with this, you'd better say so.
I'll understand.' His voice was gentle, but the
kindness hurt her too. It was the kindness he might
show to a total stranger who seemed upset.

'No, it's OK,' she said. If his script showed her a
distorted image of herself, she would have to learn to
forget it was meant to be her. He was right.

'Sure?'

'Yes. Shall we get on with it?' she said, her fingers
poised over the keys.

'It isn't you, Suzy,' Liam said roughly, walking
towards her. 'Get that through your head! It isn't you
at all! It's a girl I invented, a mask I put on your face.

If there's anything of you in the script it was only borrowed to flesh out another character.'

'Yes; it doesn't matter,' she said shortly. She did not want him to talk about this other self of hers who he now pretended was not her: this unrecognisable, familiar image he had conjured up to help erase his own pain and guilt. Suzy felt like someone who has wandered into a fairground hall of mirrors and sees herself reflected everywhere—herself and yet not herself, but a dancing line of shifting, wavering, deceiving shapes that dissolved from one to the other endlessly. She was lost and confused. That isn't me, she kept telling herself, that can't be me.

Yet wasn't the most terrible part of it the fact that she *did* get fleeting glimpses of her real self in those mirrors? Liam had caught her in words: a flash of her here, another there. She came and went among the false images, disorientating her own mind, confusing and bewildering and hurting her.

They broke for tea a short time later and then resumed work quite soon. By the end of the afternoon they had reached the end of the written manuscript Liam had brought to her office.

'That's wonderful,' he said, flicking over her immaculate pages. 'I should certainly finish the script by the time Stevenson gets back, at this rate.'

Suzy stood up, rather tired after so much concentrated effort, and Liam frowned at her.

'You're pale. Tired?'

'A little.'

'Look, let me get you some supper before you go. I cook a decent risotto—that was what I'd planned to have; chicken and mushrooms and green peppers.'

'No, really——' she began, but he took her coat from her and threw it down on a chair again.

'Sit down, Suzy; relax in front of the TV while I cook the risotto.'

'I don't feel like TV,' she said, her eyes wandering to his rows of bookshelves, and he gestured to them.

'Help yourself—but stay in that chair until the meal is ready.'

He went out and she looked after him, hesitating; tempted yet wary. Well, why not? she thought, shrugging fatalistically. She was dead on her feet and didn't feel like fighting her way across London in the rush hour. She walked along the bookshelves, picked out an illustrated travel guide to the Mediterranean and sat down with that, skipping from picture to picture and wishing she was somewhere in the sun, lazily relaxing on a beach.

When Liam came back Suzy had curled up in the chair, her feet tucked under her, her head leaning on a cushion. He stood watching her closed eyes, and Suzy suddenly woke up from the light sleep. At that second Liam's fingers brushed her blonde hair back from her face; her lids lifted and she looked at him, eyes wide, colour coming and going.

'I thought you were asleep,' he said roughly.

Flushed, she said, 'I closed my eyes for a second, that's all.'

'The risotto's ready,' he said, a tray balanced on his arm, and she stumbled to her feet.

The food was good and he served a chilled Lambrusco with it; the fizzy red wine was so light, she drank too much and only realised it was stronger than she had thought when she began to get sleepier again. Liam drove her home and she fell asleep in the passenger seat, her head against his shoulder when she woke up.

'Suzy,' he said, touching her cheek softly, and she looked drowsily at him, a peculiar heat stealing through her body. She had been dreaming of him; the passion of the dream was still in her eyes.

Liam's face grew taut, his eyes probing hers, then he frowned. 'You should be in bed,' he said, and Suzy felt herself blushing and was so horrified that she almost fell out of the car, which shot away almost the second she slammed the door.

She walked away, biting her inner lip until she tasted the salt of her own blood. She had hated the conflict of their meetings in the last few weeks, and had wished bitterly that she had never been fool enough to buy a copy of his book, and, in her damned curiosity, like Pandora opening the fatal box, let loose a swarm of troubles on her world. Now, though, she felt stupidly that she preferred Liam's hostility to this new distant courtesy. At least there had been some sort of contact between them when he snarled and sniped at her; behind his anger she had felt the harsh drag of an emotion matching her own. Now he seemed quite indifferent; he had cleared their account and all the left-over emotion he had once felt had been used up; she meant nothing to him and that realisation was painful.

It was crazy to admit that, even to herself, Suzy thought over and over again during the rest of that day and the dull, peaceful days that followed. Only a fool would prefer to be savaged by an angry man every time they met rather than exchange polite nothings over a desk with a man whose eyes were as remote as arctic regions.

Was she some kind of masochist? Or maybe she felt she had to pay off a debt owing to Mark? Perhaps she had been hugging her unhappiness for these last three years because Mark had died in a duel with Liam over her? For weeks at a time she had often managed to forget all about Mark, but if anything recalled him to her mind she would feel the same stab of guilt and pain each time.

Death had such icy finality. However many times she told herself it wasn't her fault, she had never quite managed to convince herself, because she was alive and Mark was dead. Liam's bitterness towards her had been what she expected, what she secretly felt she deserved. Mark would always have come between her and Liam; dead, he was more of a barrier than he had been when he was alive.

CHAPTER TEN

As Suzy slid into the routine of taking a taxi every afternoon to Liam's flat to work with him, she expected to become accustomed to his presence; she hoped her heart would beat regularly when he smiled at her and her pulses would stay steady, but, maddeningly, familiarity did not breed contempt, nor did custom make the slightest impression on her crazy metabolism. Every time he opened the door to her she felt her heart miss a beat; every time he spoke in that deep, velvety voice her ears seemed to sing; every time he smiled at her, her pulses hammered like a whole orchestra of drummers.

Of course, she struggled never to let him guess. Liam had told her brusquely that he no longer hated her, and by that he meant she was of no interest to him at all, apart from her function as a secretary who could take dictation fast enough for him to be able to write his script aloud while he paced backwards and forwards in the room; hardly aware of her, she sensed. She had become an extension of himself, her fingers on the typewriter moving to his mind's command. He argued out his thoughts to her and needed no answer from her. Suzy instinctively knew better than to answer; that would have broken the spell, made him aware of her.

'No, I don't think he'd say that,' he would mutter.

'I think he'd just turn round and walk away, don't you?'

Dumb, Suzy sat, fingers poised.

'What did she say?' Liam came up behind her, putting his hands on her shoulders as he leant over to glance at the page in the typewriter, and Suzy tried not to tremble, hoping he couldn't hear the fierce drag of her breathing. Liam was repeating the last few lines he had written, saying the words in a low, rapid mutter. He seemed totally oblivious of the brush of her hair on his cheek, but Suzy was violently aware of it.

'OK,' he said, straightening, and began his pacing again, picking up where he had left off.

It was only very gradually that Suzy began to realise how the storyline was changing; it was an imperceptible change at first, a new angle on a scene at one moment, something said by one of the three major characters shortly afterwards. She registered them and then slowly noticed more and more of them. The script was very different from the novel, which was only to be expected, of course—but it was more than the usual difference involved in a transfer from one medium to another; it was a radical change in emphasis. Liam was still building the story on the love triangle, but it was no longer the sharply defined black and white caricature of herself she was reading. Liam was giving other perspectives of that girl she both knew and did not recognise. He was deepening the picture of the girl, changing her in ways which made her far less like Suzy and at the same time gave a far more sympathetic and less biased portrait.

At first, Suzy couldn't quite put her finger on how he was achieving this, but then it dawned on her—the girl had begun to speak to herself. In the novel the girl had only been seen through the eyes of the two men in love with her; she had been the catalyst, the cause of the tragedy that wrecked the men's lives. Liam had made no effort to look at the situation through her eyes or ask himself how she had felt, his view of her had been too angry.

In the script, however, he was looking at what had happened from all three angles—the triangle was complete and far more human. Liam blamed none of the entangled trio now, and that gave his script far more depth and far more power.

The relief and happiness which filled Suzy as she recognised the very different emphasis in the script had to be hidden—she couldn't bear to say anything to Liam. She was afraid of saying the wrong thing, of altering in some way the whole balance of his attitude, causing a return of the hostility which had been such a painful aspect of the novel but which she no longer saw in the script.

Liam usually stopped dictating at around five-thirty. The pages mounted up for the first hour, then he would go back and start rewriting, throwing away what he had just done, so that by the end of the day they were lucky to end up with eight or nine typed pages. The script would be around a hundred pages long in the end and at that pace they should have finished it by the time Alex got back, Suzy thought one evening, as she got up from the typewriter, flexing her fingers wearily.

'I hope this isn't too tiring,' said Liam, frowning.

'Oh, no,' she said quickly, desperately hunting for something more to add, but unable to come up with anything. Her brain always seemed to go on strike when Liam was near her. She looked at her watch. 'My taxi should be here soon.' She had got into the habit of ordering one to pick her up at a quarter to six each evening.

'Heard from Stevenson?' asked Liam, putting down the pile of typed pages he had been glancing through. 'I had two cards this morning, by the same post, covered with tiny scribbled messages. Probably very helpful about the script—if I could have read any of it.'

Suzy laughed involuntarily. 'I can translate Alex's scribble quite easily now, but it had me foxed for quite a while—do you want me to have a shot at reading the cards?'

'Would you?' Liam walked over to a wall cabinet and hunted through a pile of letters, turning with the gaily coloured postcards in his hand.

Suzy took them and studied them ruefully for a moment or two before she could pick out most of Alex's messages. As Liam had guessed, Alex had sent him advice about the script, and when she read this out Liam grimaced. Sunlight gave the sharp contours of his face a breathtaking incision; his features were so strong and clear-cut. Yet it was the warm, relaxed curve of his mouth her gaze lingered on. She couldn't believe he was smiling at her like that—really smiling again. It was a small miracle.

'I don't think I can take any more advice at the

moment. I've enough trouble trying to keep my dialogue to a minimum and still get in most of what the characters have to say. It's a damned sight harder than I'd expected.'

'Yes. So much of film is visual.'

'I know, Carina kept rubbing that in.'

Suzy looked down, very still. 'I thought you would have gone on working with her,' she suggested tentatively, very curious about why Liam had not done that.

'She's a clever woman,' Liam said drily, 'but she does like to run the whole show, doesn't she? I had a feeling that if I agreed to let her co-write, I'd find her name on my script by the time it was finished.'

Suzy smiled. 'Carina's ambitious.'

'You can say that again! The lady makes no secret of it, which is fine with me, but I'm ambitious too, and this is my book, my script.' Suzy wasn't surprised to hear him say all that; she had always known that there was a ruthless streak in Liam. How else could he have won race after race during his years on the track?

They both heard the blare of a horn outside. 'Your taxi,' Liam said casually, and she gave a suppressed sigh as she moved towards the door. Her time with him seemed to slip by much too fast; she wanted it to stretch out to the crack of doom.

They finished the script on the Thursday before Alex was due back, and to celebrate Liam invited her to have dinner with him that evening, in the Chinese restaurant below his flat. The family who ran it made a big fuss of Liam and Suzy when they walked in, and, although the restaurant was quite busy, found them a good table by the window, lit the tiny red Chinese lantern on the table and brought some fresh flowers, the white heads of daisies floating on a flat green glass saucer. Suzy felt a glow of warmth as she and Liam talked and considered the enormous menu. Both of them had a sense of achievement tonight; they had worked hard while Alex was away and they both felt that the script was not at all bad. Spending an evening together in these quiet, civilised surroundings was the perfect ending for these weeks.

'Lobster balls and broccoli in ginger,' Liam suggested.

'Duck in orange sauce,' she countered, and his brows flew up.

'As well? Good grief, woman, your digestion must be amazing. One or the other, but not both!'

The proprietor brought them an enormous mixture of dishes in little white bowls and while they picked out what they liked Liam told her about the visit he had made to Hong Kong—working on an English newspaper part-time, visiting mainland China, writing his novel, learning some Chinese and enjoying the wide variety of food you could find.

'I loved it there,' Suzy said, and told him in her turn about the trip she had made there with Alex. She went on to talk about Alex's sudden illness, the shock and fear she and Sara had felt as they sat together at his bedside. 'Alex is always so . . . oh, vital! It didn't even look like him in that bed. It's taken him ages to get over it.'

'When do you think he'll start shooting my film?' asked Liam.

'Impossible to say.' Suzy felt herself tightening up; she knew Alex wouldn't forgive her if she told Liam too much. It might be two years before they actually started shooting, or even longer; it might be in six months. Luck had a lot to do with it, but Liam wouldn't appreciate being told that.

Liam filled her glass, his mouth hard. 'OK, sorry I asked. I'll tackle Stevenson when he gets back.' He lifted his own glass, tilting it towards her in a polite toast. 'Thanks for all your hard work, I'm very grateful.'

Suzy smiled waveringly. 'I enjoyed it, and thank you for this lovely dinner.' It had been a special evening, her mind had drunk in images of Liam smiling, his grey eyes wry as he described some street in Hong Kong where you could spend a fortune on jade or ivory in shops which looked as if they sold nothing but junk. 'You can't go by appearances,' he had said drily, and their eyes had met, Suzy's wide with shock and Liam's cool.

'That wasn't a dig at you,' he had said flatly, reading her expression, and she had looked down, fighting for self-control. Liam had gone on talking and she hadn't glanced up again for some time, but whenever she remembered that moment she felt the same chill realisation. Liam's bitter anger had gone and with it every trace of feeling towards her. Only a short time ago she wouldn't have believed it possible for them to sit in a restaurant politely exchanging their views of the most popular play in the West End at the moment, or talking quietly about the film-making process. Liam was naturally fascinated by it, since he was about to discover it personally, and asked Suzy a series of questions, listening intently to her answers.

Any outsider, seeing them together, might well have imagined that they barely knew each other, she realised bleakly. Well, in a sense that was true; they were both very different people from the lovers who had parted in violence three years ago.

Joshua rang her on Friday morning, burbling excitedly. 'Guess what, you'll never guess!'

'What?' she asked, smiling at his boyishly eager voice.

'I did it! And she said yes! Suzy, she said yes! I couldn't believe it, and I just sat there like a dummy with my mouth open, but she meant it. We're getting married right away—Linda doesn't want an engagement. Will you come to the wedding?'

'Are you asking me to be best man?' teased Suzy, and he chuckled. 'I'm very pleased for you, Joshua,' she added seriously. 'It's wonderful news, I hope you and Linda will be very happy.'

'We're going to be,' he said with confidence. 'Linda thinks we ought to live in her flat because it's bigger than mine.'

Suzy listened wryly as he reeled off a list of all the other decisions Linda had made for them both—why hadn't Linda proposed to him months ago? she wondered. She obviously intended to make all his other arrangements for him, but as Joshua seemed more than happy with that, no doubt the marriage would be ecstatically happy. Linda was a clever, ambitious woman and Joshua was a malleable man; they made a better match than Suzy had ever realised until now. Linda would organise Joshua's life for him far more efficiently than he had ever done.

Putting down the phone, she swung round in her chair and gazed out of the window; it was raining and the sky had an ominous lividity as if the clouds would not be moving for a long time. Alex and Sara were probably back by now. They had been flying overnight and would go straight to their London flat, because Leah intended to have this party for them on the Saturday night, so there would be no point in driving down to Kent until after the party.

Suzy didn't expect to hear from them today. After an all-night flight they would be suffering from jet lag, no doubt.

She watched the rain running down the windows, sighing. If Liam was at the party would he come with Carina? Suzy didn't know if she could stand watching them together, dancing, their arms around each other. She closed her eyes, biting her lip, and at that second a pair of hands fastened over her eyes.

She jumped with a yelp of shock and spun round.

Alex grinned at her, sitting down on the edge of her desk. 'Is this how you've been occupying yourself while I've been away? Daydreaming?'

'You scared the life out of me, sneaking up like that!' she gasped, then stared wide-eyed. 'You're so brown! You look like a gingerbread man!'

'I began to feel like one,' Alex said drily. 'I baked and baked on a beach for days on end. Sara was remorseless; she wouldn't let me do anything except swim and sunbathe, and only allowed me a little light reading.'

Suzy was amused, watching his suntanned, lively face. Alex was quite himself again; he looked fit and buzzing with energy.

'Like the gingerbread man, I rebelled in the end and threatened to run as fast as I could all the way back to wet, gloomy, wonderful London,' Alex told her, grimacing. 'So she relented and we did a little island-hopping in a rented boat. It wasn't until I was on the plane coming home that it dawned on me that Sara had still managed to keep me too occupied to think or read.' He leaned towards her. 'Women are born tyrants.'

'You obviously had a fabulous holiday,' said Suzy, unimpressed by his complaints, and he laughed, nodding.

'We did—but now I'm dying to get back to work. Has Moor finished a draft of the script?'

She nodded. 'I've typed it for him and I kept a copy for you.' She went to the filing cabinet and fished out the folder holding the script. Alex had followed her over there and was waiting eagerly, his hand held out. Wryly, Suzy handed it to him and he at once began flicking through the pages, his face intent. Watching him, she saw satisfaction in those hard eyes.

'This is good,' he said, looking up. 'Carina's a terrific tutor; she obviously worked hard with Liam.'

Suzy's mouth stiffened and she walked back to her desk without answering. Alex seemed to have forgotten her own very personal involvement with Liam; she had no intention of reminding him of it, but it wasn't easy to listen to him talking about Liam and she was tempted to repeat to him what Liam had said about Carina, resenting Carina's desire to take over his script.

'Well, I won't go through the letters and memos with you now; we'll leave that for Monday,' said Alex, strolling to the door. 'I'll take the script with me and concentrate on that for the moment.' He opened the door, then looked back. 'How are you getting to the party tomorrow night? Can we give you a lift? Or is someone else taking you?'

'I'd be grateful for a lift, if it's no trouble,' Suzy said, and Alex told her he would pick her up at her flat at seven the following night.

She did not want to go to Leah Jonas's party, but her pride wouldn't let her make an excuse to cancel. Instead, she went out and bought herself a new and very expensive dress: a formal black silk with an off-the-shoulder, ruched bodice held up by the tiniest straps, a tight waist with a silver rose pinned at the centre and a full, stiff skirt that swished satisfyingly as she walked. It was rather more daring that the dresses she usually wore, but she knew the sort of competition she would have at Leah's party. She would probably be the only woman there who couldn't afford to wear Leah's designs.

She started to get ready very early. By five-thirty she was soaking in a scented bath, her face glowing after it had been vitalised by an avocado face pack. Her body relaxed, silken and smooth in the foaming water, but her mind refused to do likewise. She was dreading the next few hours and didn't know how she

was going to be able to get through them. She had a
sick suspicion that tonight she would know for
certain; she would be able to tell, when she saw them
together, whether or not Liam and Carina were
having an affair. You couldn't hide it; it showed in
your eyes, in the way you looked at each other. Suzy
despised herself for her cowardice, but she would
rather not be sure. She didn't want to have to face it.

As she was reluctantly stepping out of the bath she
heard the doorbell, and was startled. Alex? It couldn't
be, it was far too early. Or had he decided to arrive
before anyone else to talk to L.J. about Liam's script?

She wouldn't put that past him; it was the sort of
impulsive decision Alex did take. Suzy grimaced and
towelled herself lightly before slipping into a short
white robe. If it was Alex and Sara, they would either
have to go on without her or come in and wait while
she got dressed.

'You're early,' she said, pulling open the door—
then froze, staring blankly at Liam.

'Stevenson asked me to pick you up,' he said in the
quiet tones he had been using over the past three
weeks while they worked together. 'He wanted to
have a long talk with Mr Jonas before the party, and
he's already down there.'

Suzy bit down on her lip, her eyes skating away.
She had been partly right in her guesswork; Alex had
done just as she suspected. What she hadn't thought
of was that he might send someone else to collect her,
or that it might be Liam.

Anger burned inside her as she hesitated. How
could Alex be so thoughtless? Had he completely

forgotten why she wouldn't want Liam to take her to the party? Or didn't he care?

'I'm not dressed yet,' she muttered huskily, unable to meet Liam's eyes.

His voice was dry. 'I'll wait.' He was in evening dress; it looked far too good on him. Suzy tried not to notice too much as she moved back to let him walk into her flat. She must not be so aware of how he looked; it was dangerous to her peace of mind.

'I can always get a taxi,' she suggested, still hesitating. 'I don't want to be a problem—why don't you go on and . . .'

'I wanted to talk to you anyway,' Liam interrupted, and she glanced up, then, her blue eyes wide in surprise.

'What about?'

He was frowning, his black brows a heavy line above his eyes. 'Can we sit down for a second?' he asked, as if he was about to give her bad news, but she couldn't imagine what he could have to say that might be such a shock to her that she had to sit down to hear it. Then her heart turned over and an icy coldness washed over her skin as it occurred to her that he might be going to tell her he was going to marry Carina.

Silently, she turned and walked into the sitting-room and sat down, her hands clasped in her lap to hide their tell-tale trembling. Liam sat down a few feet away, watching her with what she recognised as compassion. Her throat burned with pain; he was sorry for her, he knew he was about to tell her news that would hurt her, which meant that Liam realised she still cared for him. The humiliation of that was almost worse than the misery of waiting to hear what he had to say. She felt that she could almost wish Liam wanted to hurt her; that would be preferable to pity.

'There's something I think you ought to know before you go to the party,' he said in a rough voice. 'There's going to be an announcement tonight—someone's getting married.'

Suzy held her head up, her neck rigid, her mouth stiff, fighting to look calm. She would not show emotion. Her blue eyes darkened defiantly as she met Liam's watchful stare.

'Alex just told me,' Liam said harshly, and Suzy stared in bewilderment as the words sank in. 'He didn't appear to realise it would mean anything to you,' he added, 'but I remembered the name of the guy I've seen you around with and I guessed that . . .'

'Joshua and Linda?' Suzy burst out, suddenly catching on to what he was talking about, and Liam nodded, watching her intently. She began to laugh then, a laughter which had a wild edge to it because of her deep relief that Liam hadn't been talking about himself.

'If you don't want to go to the party now . . .' he began, and she sobered, looking at him with a wry little smile.

'Of course I want to go to the party! I've known that Joshua was going to marry Linda for ages.'

Liam's brows met, his grey eyes hardening. 'And you still dated him?'

She flushed at the contempt in his voice. 'I've never

dated Joshua, not the way you mean. He's a friend, no more than that. He and Linda have been a pair for months.'

'That wasn't the impression I got! I thought you and he . . .'

'You jumped to conclusions.' Suzy got to her feet and headed for the door, but didn't reach it. Liam grabbed her and wrenched her round to face his accusing eyes. Her heart sank. This is where I came in, she thought bleakly. Liam is hating me again; his calm politeness was skin deep. The first chance it gets, the old hatred leaps out again.

'Don't lie to me again!' he snarled, shaking her. 'I heard him with my own ears, so don't try to kid me he wasn't interested in you. I walked into your office one day and he was asking you if he had a chance. He may not have been offering marriage, but he was certainly after something from you.'

The cynical twist of his mouth made her furious. Her face burning, she eyed him defiantly. 'Advice,' she snapped. 'That's what he wanted from me, advice! He wasn't talking about me, he was talking about Linda. He wanted to know if I thought he had a chance with her—he was afraid to propose in case she turned him down.'

Liam stared down into her angry eyes, his grip on her shoulder slowly relaxing. The locked bones of his face unclenched too; she saw the tension and rage draining out of him.

'He asked you if he ought to propose to another woman?' Liam sounded incredulous, and Suzy's grimace admitted she agreed with his disbelief.

'Well, Joshua isn't exactly strong-minded. He's a "come and move me, Mother, I'm burning" type. That's why he needs someone like Linda. She knows exactly what she's doing, and she'll manage Joshua as well as her own life.'

Liam's fixed gaze probed her face. 'And you aren't upset?'

'About Joshua and Linda? No, of course not. I told you, he's just a friend . . .'

Liam's hand was moving slowly, stroking and absently fondling her shoulder while he watched her, and Suzy suddenly felt a pang of alarm. What was going on inside that head of his as he looked at her like that? Her eyes darkened and she clutched the neck of her robe together with a shaky hand, moving away.

'I'd better go and get dressed.'

'Plenty of time,' said Liam, his voice very deep and husky. 'We don't have to get to the party for hours yet.'

Suzy was distinctly nervous now; she backed, afraid to take her eyes off him in case he pounced, intensely conscious of him and feeling rather like someone cornered by a hungry tiger. If there had been a tree around, Suzy would have climbed it. As it was she kept taking another step backwards towards the door, and Liam kept moving after her, a sardonic glitter in his eyes.

'It didn't work,' he murmured. 'I suppose I knew all along that I was kidding myself.'

'What are you talking about?' Suzy had almost got to the door now and was debating whether it was time to make a run for it to her bedroom. Liam's legs were much longer than hers; he would probably beat her to it and she had absolutely no wish to find herself trapped in a bedroom with him when he looked like that.

'You know what I mean,' he said softly. 'We could never become strangers, never in a million years. I tried to tell myself I could see you marrying another man without wanting to kill the pair of you, but I was lying to myself.'

A stab of sweet pain made her bite down on her lip, but she was afraid of listening to him, afraid this was another twist of his revenge on her. If she admitted she still loved him, Liam might turn and rend her, and she didn't think she would survive any more torture at his hands.

She shook her head. 'Don't talk like that. It's all over. You'd better go.' Somehow she found the courage to walk to the front door and open it and, after a brief surprised pause, Liam followed her. Suzy stood there, holding the door, her eyes lowered. She couldn't look at him; it had taken the last ounce of her strength to resist the temptation he had just held out.

'Look at me!' His finger pushed her chin forcibly upwards and her darkened eyes met his; Liam stared searchingly into her face while she trembled, her mouth too dry for speech.

A moment later she was being lifted up into his arms. Liam kicked the front door shut and carried her down the corridor to her bedroom.

She turned her face into his chest, whispering pleadingly, 'Don't do this to me, Liam, please don't.'

He laid her on her bed and knelt beside her, his

mouth hunting for hers as she turned her head away, desperately trying to avoid his kiss.

'It wouldn't work, you know it wouldn't,' she whispered. 'We'd never be able to forget Mark, what happened—we'd be haunted and in the end we might hate each other again. I couldn't bear it, Liam!'

He softly bit her ear and she closed her eyes, the tiny pain intensely pleasurable.

'If we'd got married three years ago, just after it happened, you would have been right. It took me all this time to come to terms with my own responsibility for Mark's death. I was running from it rather than face it, and I blamed you because I couldn't blame myself and I was afraid to blame Mark. I was full of anger and bitterness; it was a sort of despair, and despair is a deadly sin, Suzy. It doesn't admit of forgiveness and human understanding; it doesn't accept that we're all fallible and all capable of mistakes. The coroner's inquest had the right verdict. Mark's death was an accident. He didn't mean to die—it wasn't his intention when we had that race. He lost his temper and he wanted to beat me, prove he was the better man, hit me hard where he thought it would hurt most. I didn't kill Mark, nor did you. We didn't cause his death; we merely fell in love, and Mark couldn't take it—he wouldn't let you go because he hated losing anything.'

Suzy lay very still, listening, her face averted, but deeply aware of his lips moving against her neck as he murmured to her. His warm breath touched her skin and the warmth seemed to spread downwards through layers of frozen pain, thawing her heart.

'But he didn't love me,' she said flatly.

'No, I don't think he ever did. He wasn't adult enough to love anyone else. That was his mother's fault; she spoilt him.' Liam undid the belt of her robe and she stiffened as she felt his hand slide exploringly under the material.

'Stop that!' she muttered hoarsely, pushing his hand away, but she made the fatal error of looking up at him as she protested.

She only got a fleeting glimpse of his darkly flushed face as his head swooped down; then he took her mouth, his lips so hot and ruthless that she had no hope of resisting them, her own lips almost at once beginning to kiss him back.

Liam touched her naked body and she moaned, eyes shut, weak with desire and yielding to the caressing movements of his fingers.

'I love you, Suzy,' he muttered as she fumbled with the buttons on his shirt. 'Even more now than I did in the beginning. It's cost us so much, hurt so much, but it's still there, stronger then ever. It's the same for you, isn't it?'

There was the faintest uncertainty in his voice and she smiled with quivering lips as she pushed his shirt away and burrowed into his naked skin, her mouth nibbling and sucking. She wanted to taste him, absorb him, consume him, love him.

'What?' asked Liam, unable to make sense of what she was groaning against his throat.

'I love you,' Suzy said unsteadily. 'Darling, stop talking and make love to me; you're driving me crazy!'

He laughed in his throat with a rough purring and hurriedly pulled off the rest of his clothes while she lay watching him through half-closed lids, her ears singing with blood pressure and her body shaking with urgent necessity. As he came down on her she heard the cry she gave and shut her eyes, startled by her own lack of inhibition.

He was the only lover she had ever had, and it was three years since they had made love, yet her body arched up and opened to receive him as if he belonged inside her and should never have left. She was shuddering from head to foot as he moved on her and in her, her arms holding him closer, her thighs gently stroking against his with a teasing friction that urged him on, her head turning from side to side on the pillow in restless excitement.

When she began to give the gasping little cries of pleasure, she heard Liam groan thickly, his head buried on her breast, but a second later Suzy was unaware even of him; her head thrown back and her teeth clenched, she went through wave after wave of piercing sweetness until she lay still, breathing as if she had been running.

Liam looked down at her wryly as her lids stirred and she shyly risked a glance at him.

'Well, well, well! You were in a hurry,' he mocked.

'Three years is a long time,' she said, laughing a little unsteadily.

'You might have waited for me,' Liam murmured, but he was smiling and his eyes held a promise that made Suzy smile back, her hands running along his muscled arms and shoulders to stroke his neck and delve into the thick, crisp hair.

'We have plenty of time,' she whispered.

'Do you think L.J. will notice if we don't turn up at his party?'

'We can always arrive late and say we got caught in traffic.'

Liam bent and ran his tongue tip along her lip. 'Brilliant; I'm sure they'll believe us implicitly. One look at us and the whole room will know what we've been doing!'

Suzy moved lazily against his powerful body, her thigh curving against him while her hands slowly ran down his spine and pressed him closer. 'I don't care what they think. I don't care what anybody thinks, so long as you love me.'

His face was intent and very serious; his grey eyes watched her with passion and deep feeling.

'I love you, Suzy,' he said almost flatly. 'I've loved you almost from the minute we first met. I never stopped and I never will.'

She closed her eyes, pulling him down towards her. 'Show me.'

Harlequin Presents

Coming Next Month

Available in January wherever paperback books are sold, or through Harlequin Reader Service:

In the U.S.
901 Fuhrmann Blvd.
P.O. Box 1397
Buffalo, N.Y. 14240-1397

In Canada
P.O. Box 603
Fort Erie, Ontario
L2A 5X3

Harlequin Intrigue

In October
Watch for the new look of

Harlequin Intrigue
... because romance can be quite an adventure!

Each time, Harlequin Intrigue brings you great stories, mixing a contemporary, sophisticated romance with the surprising twists and turns of a puzzler... romance with "something more."

Plus...
in next month's publications of Harlequin Intrigue we offer you the chance to win one of four mysterious and exciting weekends. Don't miss the opportunity! Read the October Harlequin Intrigues!

An enticing
new historical romance!

Spring
Will Come
SHERRY DeBorde

It was 1852, and the steamy South was in its last hours of gentility. Camille Braxton Beaufort went searching for the one man she knew she could trust, and under his protection had her first lesson in love....

Available in October at your favorite retail outlet, or reserve your copy for September shipping by sending your name, address, zip or postal code, along with a check or money order for $4.70 (includes 75¢ postage and handling) payable to Worldwide Library to:

In the U.S.	In Canada
Worldwide Library	Worldwide Library
901 Fuhrmann Blvd.	P.O. Box 609
P.O. Box 1325	Fort Erie, Ontario
Buffalo, NY 14269-1325	L2A 5X3

Please specify book title with your order.

 WORLDWIDE LIBRARY

SPR-1

ATTRACTIVE, SPACE SAVING BOOK RACK

Display your most prized novels on this handsome and sturdy book rack. The hand-rubbed walnut finish will blend into your library decor with quiet elegance, providing a practical organizer for your favorite hard-or soft-covered books.

Only $9.95

Approximately 16" x 8" when assembled

Assembles in seconds!

To order, rush your name, address and zip code, along with a check or money order for $10.70* ($9.95 plus 75¢ postage and handling) payable to *Harlequin Reader Service*:

> Harlequin Reader Service
> Book Rack Offer
> 901 Fuhrmann Blvd.
> P.O. Box 1396
> Buffalo, NY 14269-1396

Offer not available in Canada.

BKR-1A

*New York and Iowa residents add appropriate sales tax.

Coming Soon
from Harlequin . . .

GIFTS FROM THE HEART

**Watch for it
in February**